A Brief Moment of Weightlessness

A Brief Moment of Weightlessness

Stories by Victoria Fish

Mayapple Press 2014

Published by   MAYAPPLE PRESS
                 362 Chestnut Hill Rd.
                 Woodstock, NY 12498
                 www.mayapplepress.com

ISBN 978-1-936419-40-1
Library of Congress Control Number: 2014937497

ACKNOWLEDGMENTS

Bloodroot: Sanctuary Therapy; *Cell 2 Soul:* Between the Dream and
Here; *Hunger Mountain:* Phantom Pain; *Literary Mama:* Unleashed;
Quality Women's Fiction: The Voice At the End of the Line (titled
"Beads"); *Slow Trains:* The Sari.

I couldn't have written word one without the love and support of
my husband, Hugh Huizenga, and my three boys, Andrew, Noah and
Peter. They truly gave me room to write, and I love them all beyond
words. The stories here would never have become a collection without
the faith and patronage of my mother, Imogene Fish. I want extend
deep gratitude to Joni Cole and all the writers at the Writers Center
of White River Junction, Vermont, for perceptive reading, thoughtful
criticism and constant encouragement. Thank you to Eric Rickstad
for his help in shaping this collection and to Judy Kerman at Mayapple
Press for making the idea of this book a reality.

Cover photo by Jon Olsen. Cover designed by Judith Kerman. Book designed
and typeset by Amee Schmidt with titles in Hypatia and text in Californian FB.
Author photo courtesy of Tracy Koehler.

Contents

Where Do You Find a Turtle with No Legs?

The shell of the flattened turtle looked like the tile in the bathroom at the county jail, where Maddie threw up the first time she visited her dad. The turtle looked freshly squished. Maddie poked it with the toe of her blue Keds just to see. The turtle had almost made it to the side of the road when its back legs got rolled over by a car. It was so sad. Were there baby turtles waiting in the woods for her to come back? Maddie just knew the turtle was a her.

She wanted to touch the turtle, but Ranger Sandra who visited their 4th grade class once a month as part of Nature's Classroom warned the students about animal germs and the importance of hand washing. Maddie squatted down, and the pavement breathed heat up on the back of her legs. The turtle's head was so small compared with its enormous shell. The turtle was way longer than her foot and the shell was at least ten times as big—for the turtle—as her backpack pushing down on her back was for her. Would the baby turtles be hungry without their mother? Would a turtle make a good pet? Maddie stood up and walked over to the high grasses at the side of the road and peered.

Every year she wrote on her birthday *and* Christmas lists: *Kitten; Puppy.* But her mom said dogs were too much work and money, and her dad was allergic to cats. Still. Just one little pet, that's all Maddie wanted. She loved how dogs ran to the door to greet you. She liked the thought of a cat curling up in her lap, completely content. Even a turtle would look right at you with its little slivers of eyes, happy you were there to feed it and love it. Her sister Lizbeth said, "You are obsessed." The way Lizbeth said the word *obsessed* made it sound annoying, which was weird because Maddie'd heard Lizbeth on the phone telling Randy, "I am obsessed with you."

Maddie picked up a stick and parted the long grasses to see if there was a nest of baby turtles anywhere. *Why did the turtle cross the road?* Her dad loved jokes like this. Sometimes her mom warned, "Inappropriate, Frank!" when he "crossed the line." He'd crossed the line a lot more this past year, after getting laid off from his job. Maddie's mom said the tallboys didn't help. Maddie decided to polish up a few jokes for the next time they visited her dad.

"What're you doing?" Lizbeth said as her bike brakes shrieked, and she stopped her bike just inches from the turtle. "Ew. Gross," she said and blew a pink bubble the size of a fist, opened her mouth wide to suck the bubble back in before it popped on her face.

"It's not gross. It's sad," Maddie said.

Lizbeth was wearing the super-short cut-off blue jeans and the pink spaghetti-strapped tank top that showed her bra straps and even the top of her boobs. "Mom told you not to wear that to school today," Maddie said. Their mother had said, "Are you kidding me? Don't you think people in this town are talking already?" Lizbeth shouted, "You think people will be talking about *me*?" Their mom's face went white, and she backed into the bathroom.

"You gonna tell on me?" Lizbeth pursed her glossy pink lips and bumped her front tire lightly into the turtle.

"Stop it!" Maddie said, pointing her stick at Lizbeth.

"Whatever. Listen. Get your butt home when you're done crying over this thing. Mom's gonna call soon, and she'll be pissed if we're not there." Their mom was a nurse at the hospital, where Goddard lay in his coma. She usually worked the noon to eight p.m. shift, Mondays through Fridays. She always tried to call them when she thought they should be home from school, especially Fridays, since she worried about Lizbeth heading out to party. Lizbeth pushed off on her bike with her toe. Maddie watched her sister's long shiny legs spin and then saw Lizbeth briefly lift both hands off the handle bars and high into the air, her arms like a bird's wings.

"When I'm fourteen," Maddie vowed, "I will not dress so that my private parts are flapping in the wind." Maddie stepped to the side of the road while a car passed, barely missing the turtle. She knew she shouldn't touch the turtle, but she couldn't leave it there to get squished and squished again. She pushed the stick against the back of the turtle's shell, but the stick bent and cracked and she tossed it into the grass. She'd need to touch it with her hands. She'd just wash them super good when she got home, and she wouldn't scratch her nose or touch her lips or anything with her fingers until then.

The underside of the turtle's belly was smooth against her fingers. The turtle was heavier than she thought it would be, and it was still warm. The shell reminded her of horse hoofs and army helmets and pictures she'd seen of Indian pottery with beautiful designs. *What were you thinking, turtle?* Maddie gently set the turtle in the deep grasses off the road.

Maybe turtles didn't think. Like Daddy, who always said, "You're our thinker, Maddie." *Stupid turtle, what were you thinking?*

Maybe a turtle wouldn't be such a good pet. She brushed her hands against each other then rubbed them on the ground to clean them and started walking.

Lizbeth's bike was leaning against the porch, and Maddie could see where the tires made a snake shaped path through the grass, which hadn't been mowed for two weeks. The grass was almost up to the first step, and Maddie wondered if Mrs. Dickson across the street was mad because she had to look at their yard. Mrs. Dickson was always outside, a pink gauzy scarf over her curlers, trimming up her lawn with her push mower. Mrs. Dickson probably thought the swing set was an eyesore, too. One night during the winter, a tree limb had snapped off—Maddie had woken up scared of the sound of wind singing through the windows and had put her pillow over her head—and crashed onto their swing set. Daddy had hauled the limb off to the woods in the spring, but the top of the swing set was cracked, so Maddie couldn't climb on it or swing anymore.

Saturday, Maddie woke up feeling sick to her stomach. She turned on her side and pulled her bed spread up over her more tightly and rolled to face the wall, where her collection of Koala bears was lined up. She loved looking into the bears' gentle brown eyes which seemed to overflow with kindness and understanding.

"Maddie, you awake?" her mom called through the door.

Maddie pretended she was sleeping and tried to breathe deeper, like a sleeping person.

The door opened and her mom crossed the room and jiggled Maddie's shoulder. "Wake up. We're leaving in a half hour. Maddie?"

Her mom's perfume was too strong and made Maddie's tummy hurt worse.

"I don't feel good." She stared into the eyes of the Koala bear named Taffy.

Her curtains zipped open and sunlight bounced off the walls.

"Lemme see you." Her mom kneeled next to the bed and Maddie turned. Her mother's breath was warm and smelled like coffee and Lucky Strikes, but her hands were cold on Maddie's forehead. "You're fine. I'm not leaving you here." Her face was all shut, lips pursed and chewed on, eyes squinty like she couldn't take anything in and wouldn't let anything out; the rouge on her cheeks and swish of blue on her eyelids only called attention to the tightness.

"But I think I'm going to throw up." Her mouth felt greasy and saliva was building up.

"Goddamn it. Don't *you* give me a hard time." Her mother said and flung herself out of the room, slamming the door behind her.

Maddie lay in the back seat of the car with her eyes closed, listening to the annoying *scritch* of Lizbeth filing her nails. Either her mom was driving like a crazy woman or Maddie was getting sicker as they got closer to the jail. Maddie didn't dare say anything, and when her mom told her to sit up because they were going through the gates, she did. But she kept her eyes closed, so she wouldn't have to see the barbed wire coiling like a slinky around the top of the high chain link fence. The guard at the gate asked to see her mother's ID and reminded her that they'd have to go through security and not to bring in "contraband of any sort." What was contraband? Once there was a contra dance at Maddie's elementary school gym. This was before Lizbeth stopped being fun and before their dad got laid off, and Maddie remembered them all dancing and switching partners and ending up in a dizzy heap.

Her mother parked the car and said, "Roll up your windows," but then she just sat there as the car got hotter and hotter.

"Mom?" Lizbeth tucked her nail file in the glove compartment—was that contraband?—and looked back at Maddie. "You ready?" Lizbeth wasn't snapping gum today. Maddie wondered if Lizbeth would mind if she held her hand.

The low gray building reminded Maddie of a new self-storage unit just built on the edge of town. "Reclaim your space! Climate Controlled!" Her mother's arm dropped over her shoulders and pulled her close as they walked toward the building. "You can do this, Maddie," her mother said. It sounded like encouragement and a warning all wrapped up in one.

What if when the guard dumped out her mom's purse he found something, something awful and illegal and contraband and their mother got hauled away, too? Her mother stood like she was wrapped up tight in barbed wire as the man's big red hands shuffled through the contents of her purse—Tampax, a bottle of aspirin, a wad of tissue, her mother's fake leather wallet, a pink comb, a half-eaten roll of wintergreen lifesavers, and a pair of earrings still attached to the plastic backing with the price tag. *Her mother wasn't a shoplifter, was she?* Maddie prayed that the guard didn't know Maddie had peeked at her friend's test on the times tables one day in math class. She hadn't been able to see anything because Cassandra had moved her arm, but cheating was wrong no matter what. Suddenly, Maddie tingled with guilt. The guard waved them all through the metal detector after telling Lizbeth to take off her belt with the big buckle.

They followed another guard who had a gun, a walkie-talkie, and a jangle of keys hanging from his thick black belt down a long hallway to the visitors' room. The hall smelled like Ajax and body odor, and Maddie pulled her t-shirt up over her mouth and nose so she wouldn't be sick.

"Right in here, folks," the guard said, unlocking the gray metal door for them. Maddie liked his voice. *Kindly,* she guessed you could call it. She looked back through the window on the door after he shut it behind him, but he was gone.

The room had no windows, and the off-white walls were bare, though there was a small rug in one corner with some building blocks and Legos in a pile, and high up in the corner sat a TV. The tall, skinny guard in the visitors' room pointed to a table where they were to sit and wait. The plastic chairs squeaked when they pulled them out.

At one other table, a family ate fried chicken with their prisoner, an old man with tattoos up his frail arms. His visitors looked like they were his children and grandchildren, Maddie thought, with the same hunched way of gnawing on their chicken, elbows on the table, quiet. There was one boy about Maddie's age, who sat alone at another table reading, his chicken on a napkin, untouched. Maddie tilted her head, but she couldn't see what he was reading. The smell of the chicken made her queasier.

The door opened, and another guard led their father in and locked the door again.

"Daddy!" Lizbeth pushed back her chair and ran to him before Maddie and her mom could even get to their feet. Her father's face scared Maddie. He looked like the saddest man on earth. Maddie could smell her mom's perfume and food grease coming off her dad's orange jumpsuit when her dad smashed them all in a big bear hug.

Her parents sat in the plastic chairs on one of side of the table, and she and Lizbeth sat across from them. For a second, they all stared at each other. Who would talk first? *What do you say?* The boy with the book stared at them. Lizbeth slipped a package of cinnamon gum out of her back pocket, and they all took a stick.

It was weird to sit down at a table with nothing in front of them, nothing to do but talk. Next time, Maddie would bring cookies or maybe even a little puzzle they could all work on. Would they end up like that family at the other table?

"How's school? You girls helping your mother?" Daddy asked.

"Good. School's good," Maddie said, though she didn't know how she did on that last math test. And shouldn't they be talking about other things? What was it like to be in jail? How long would he be in here? What if Goddard died?

"I'm thinking of getting a job, maybe at the general store," Lizbeth said, pulling her hair out in front of her to look for split ends.

"You'd be proud of the girls, Frank," Maddie's mother said, jiggling her foot a mile a minute, her hands clasped tight like she was saying a little prayer. Shouldn't Daddy be holding her mom's hand? Maddie wondered.

"Goddard's still in a coma," her mom blurted out.

Maddie's father shook his head *no* and said, "Shh."

Was the other family looking at them? They rolled up their chicken bones in napkins and opened a Tupperware container piled high with brownies.

"Not now," her father said, putting a hand on her mother's shoulder.

But Maddie couldn't help thinking about it, that last dump day she'd been on with her dad. She'd been in the shed called One Man's Trash is Another Man's Treasure where there was a big basket that held Beanie babies, knitting projects, and a box of *World Book Encyclopedias*, though J-K-L and P-Q-R were missing, and the books smelled like moss. She really wanted the P-Q-R, so she could research pets. Her father had always let her pick one thing from the shed, and she'd been inside it trying to find P-Q-R when he banged opened the door. His head looked twice the size as usual, and his face was red and fuming.

"We're leaving. Let's go."

"But I haven't decided what I wanted."

He grabbed her arm and hauled her through the door. "NOW."

"Daddy, what?" She hit her knee on the door as he pushed her into the truck. "What's wrong, Daddy?" She felt like crying but knew he wouldn't like that. But he didn't get in the truck. A scrawny man in a yellow windbreaker was flailing toward them yelling, "Frank Pierson! You hit my truck! I saw you!" His little face was the color of skinned knees, and spit flew from his mouth. Maddie watched as her father, hands as tight as baseballs, moved toward the man, yelling, "You're a liar now, and you were a liar then, Goddard."

"I stand by what I said then, and I stand by what I'm saying now!" The man unzipped his yellow windbreaker and threw it to the ground. Her dad was twice Goddard's size. Maddie banged on the window, "Daddy!"

"I've had it with your lies, Goddard. Your lies got me fired." His arm shot back toward Maddie, finger pointing at her. "My daughter has to scrounge at the dump now!"

She rolled down the window and cried, "I don't mind!"

Goddard had a crazy look on his face and sprang toward her dad. But her father grabbed him by the shoulders, curling Goddard's rain slicker in his fists. Goddard kicked at her father's legs as he was held at arms' length, and shouted, "You're a fucking loser, Frank." Her father coiled his neck and shoulders and snapped his head forward, smashing Goddard's temple, making a sickening crack of bone on bone.

Now, her head down on the table in the jail, again and again she watched her father draw his head back and watched as Goddard dropped to the ground, then was still.

"You okay, Maddie?" her mother asked, putting her hand on Maddie's shoulder.

Maddie felt pale and woozy when she sat up. Her father stared at her.

"Tell us a joke, Maddie," Lizbeth said, taking her gum out of her mouth and folding it up in the wrapper.

Maddie stared back at her father. He still had a slight blue-green bruise just below his hairline. She closed her eyes.

"What did the kitten put on its hamburger?" she whispered.

Lizbeth rolled her eyes.

"Catsup," she whispered.

"Good one, honey." Her mom smiled and gave her a soft punch on the arm.

"Give us another," her Dad said, his stare as strong as it was when he'd got back in the truck that day and had said, "Erase this from your mind, you hear?"

The fluorescent lights buzzed overhead.

"Where do you find a turtle with no legs?"

The other family was leaving. They swept up their bones and brownie crumbs.

"Right where you left it." Maddie stared at her father.

The boy with the book slapped his book shut and crumpled up his napkin with his untouched food and threw it into the trash can by the door.

Outside, the day was unbearably bright and hot.

Her mother started the car and unrolled all the windows.

"We three have to stick together, be a team, be strong for Daddy," she said. Maddie watched her pull a cigarette from the pack she kept in the glove compartment. She inhaled so long and deep Maddie wondered if a person's lungs ever popped.

"We need to pray tonight for Daddy. And for Goddard." Smoke spiraled out her nose. "It could be awhile."

Maddie looked out the car window as they drove away. They passed houses with dogs playing outside and men mowing lawns, and swing sets that kids could actually play on without parts breaking off. From the back seat, she could see the side of her mom's face. It had that frozen smile again. She hoped she didn't grow up and be a person who didn't smile for real anymore. Her mother should just cry if she felt like it. Wouldn't that feel better than a fake smile?

Maybe her mom would let her have a cat now, since Daddy was the one allergic to them.

"Mom?"

"Mmm?"

"How about getting a cat?"

Her mom flicked her eyes up to the rearview mirror. The smile vanished.

Lizbeth turned around from the passenger seat and said, "You stupid fucking fuckwad."

Later, Maddie sat on the front steps watching a line of ants make off with the crumbs that had fallen off her peanut butter and fluff sandwich. Lizbeth pushed open the screen door with a bang and sat next to her on the steps with a bottle of Sizzling Scarlet nail polish. She stuck little wads of toilet paper between her toes. Maddie turned back to the marching ants with their boulder size crumbs. They were going into the cracks in the rotten boards. She could hear the sound of water running which meant their mother had finally decided to leave her bedroom.

"There you two are," their mom said, squinting into the bright sun as she gingerly stepped outside, as if they were the ones who'd gone back to bed in the middle of the day. Maddie kept her eyes on the ants.

"God, this grass needs mowing." Her mother lit a cigarette. "It's hot today."

Maddie heard the suck-in of breath as her mother smoked and the creak of the rocker as she sat down with a thump.

"I like that polish color, Lizbeth."

Maddie wondered how much a crumb weighed compared to an ant.

"No one's talking to me?" her mom said and poked Maddie in the back with her toe.

"I'm concentrating," Lizbeth said.

"Let's do something fun tonight, since I picked up an extra shift tomorrow."

Maddie put the rest of her sandwich down on the rotten board for the ants.

"Lizbeth, Maddie, what do you say? Daddy said, 'Make sure the girls have fun.'"

Maddie kept watching the ants. Her peanut butter and fluff sandwich was a like a mountain and the ants were starting to take it apart, bit by tiny bit.

"Like what? I might already have plans," Lizbeth said, straightening her legs to dry her toes in the sun.

"Mini golf? Bowling? Ice cream afterwards? Think about it while I see if I can mow this damn lawn."

She put out her cigarette in the can on the porch and marched to the garage, flinging it open to reveal the truck and the mower and the jumble of tools and garbage cans. Her mother pushed the mower to the middle of the long grass, right in front of the porch steps.

"Watch this, girls." She winked.

Maddie's mother yanked the starter. Then yanked again. It sputtered and a belch of black smoke came out. She kicked the mower. She put her hands in her hair and gave a little scream.

"Maybe it needs gas, Mom." Maddie wondered if her mom would really want to go bowling or to mini golf after this.

"Oh yeah." Her mother rummaged in the garage and came out with the gas can. Some gas slopped out as she filled the mower. Now there were dozens of ants, crawling up the sandwich, dismantling it. Who was in charge? Maddie liked that every ant seemed to have a job and know what to do.

Her mother grabbed the starter and yanked, practically falling backward. The second time, the mower bucked to life. Her mother lifted one hand and gave them a thumbs up. She'd barely gone five feet when it clogged and stalled.

"Darn it all." Her mother stared at it and chewed on her thumbnail.

"I cannot watch this one more second," Lizbeth said and stalked into the house on her heels, keeping her toenails up in the air.

"I think Daddy can make the blade higher," Maddie finally offered. She'd seen him adjust the thingies on the wheels to set the blade height.

"Well he's not fucking here!" Her mother kicked the mower.

The ants had dismantled the sandwich and were marching it away in an orderly line.

Monday was Ranger Sandra day at school. The 4th grade science unit was Our Own Back Yard. Maddie loved Ranger Sandra's hat and uniform and how she wasn't afraid of spiders or snakes.

Ranger Sandra set a terrarium in the middle of their circle and reached into it. Mrs. Mulligan said not to crowd, but Maddie scooched a little closer. First she pulled out a tiny, orange newt. She walked around with the newt perched like an orange question mark on her hand and let the kids all get a close up look. Then, she picked a turtle up out of the tank.

"We found this Eastern Painted Turtle in the parking lot of our building, and we're trying to *rehabilitate* it and get it back into the wild."

She put the turtle on the blue rug and it just sat there. Not a bad pet, Maddie thought. As if Ranger Sandra was reading her mind, she said, "This is a wild animal. Not a pet. At this time of year, it is very common to see turtles on roadways. Has anyone seen a turtle on the road?"

Maddie wasn't sure if a dead turtle counted.

"Turtles like to return to their 'home range' to lay their eggs. Sometimes people think they are doing the right thing by moving them from the road to be near water or in the woods. But you should just move it out of harm's way in the direction it was heading."

The turtle was so cute. Did its eyes ever blink? What did turtles eat? Did they have to live in a terrarium or could they live in a shoe box? Ranger Sandra pointed to her, "Back up a little bit, honey, so other kids get a turn."

Maddie walked home after school. She stood in her driveway looking at the long grass and the lawn mower right where her mom had left it. Lizbeth's bike was thrown down in the gravel.

Lizbeth was sitting at the kitchen table eating Oreos and drinking purple Gatorade.

"Ranger Sandra came in today with salamanders and a turtle."

"Oh, I hope you told your jokes, Mad!" Lizbeth spewed bits of Oreo all over the table.

"Did Mom call yet?" Maddie opened the fridge and pulled out the almost-empty milk and swigged from the container.

"Do your homework, thaw the sausages, and for God sakes don't spend all afternoon on the phone." Lizbeth made her voice high and cranky, like how their mom sometimes sounded.

"I'm going to mow the lawn." Maddie unscrewed her cookie and scraped the white insides out with her tongue.

"That's not a good idea." Lizbeth got a sponge and started wiping up the table. "You'll kill yourself, and I'll have to deal with the mess." She took sausages out of the freezer and put them in the fridge.

"I'll put on boots." Maddie had heard about people who'd run over their own feet.

In the closet near the back door, she found her mother's rubber boots. Her snow boots from last winter were in there too, but they were tight and hot.

She'd seen how her dad started the mower. He made it look easy, jerking his arm back just one time. Maddie took hold of the starter and pulled. She tried again. Her arm felt like it was going to be ripped out of the socket. She tried again.

Sweat was itching her whole body and her feet felt slimy in the boots. Why hadn't she worn socks? She held the clutch on the handle and pulled a couple more times. Once, she thought she heard a little cough from the mower. She started to feel tears coming. Stupid. Stupid fucking fuckwad. She hauled her foot and kicked the mower and then collapsed in the grass on her back, tears dripping down into her ears.

"Hey." Lizbeth opened the window from the upstairs bathroom and yelled out. "Maddie, don't be stupid. Let someone else do it later."

Who? Who else? The sun was bright and hot and hurt her eyes. She wiped her nose on her shirt and rolled onto her belly. The grass could grow over her, and no one would even notice.

Maddie crawled over to the mower on her hands and knees. She stood up and put her hands in place and ripped the cord with every muscle in her body. The rumble of the engine tingled her arms and the humming went right up into her brain.

She eyed the tangle of grass, the grass that made it look like no one cared, the grass that made her mom cry, the grass where Ranger Sandra said turtles could be laying eggs this very second. The mower began to stall and grind and Maddie pushed down on the handle to raise the front tires and free the blade. Her hands felt like they could shake right off her body. Her body felt like it would spin off into a thousand little pieces. Sweat curved down along her cheek. If you see a turtle, move it out of harm's way, Ranger Sandra had said. There was probably no such thing, she thought.

A Brief Moment of Weightlessness

I pressed my nose to the car window. As we neared the coast, the light became sharper, the pines scrubbier. Everything became more of what it was. I would write that down later, maybe in a poem. Our destination was a cabin on a lake in Maine, to which we returned every summer. My mother wore the keys to the cabin on a purple string around her neck, and she jingle-jangled them and hummed *"You are my sunshine."*

"I can't wait to get the boat out, catch some fish," my father said. "Frances, are you going to learn how to row the boat this summer?" he asked me. The rowboat was big and hard to maneuver, with oars as heavy as trees. My fifteen-year old sister, Rosemary, had learned how to row the previous summer.

"Maybe," I said, eyeing Rosemary, sprawled in the back seat next to me, filing her nails into sharp little points.

"Could you stop rattling those keys, Anita?" my father said to Mom. He caught my eye in the rearview mirror, then reached over and gave my mother's knee a pat.

"I'm just excited." My mom squinted at him then turned to me and Rosemary. "It's going to be a great week, isn't it, girls?"

Rosemary grunted.

"Give me an adjective and an adverb!" I said. I was doing *Mad Libs*.

"Asinine. Pathetically," Rosemary said.

I stared at her. Her cut-off shorts were so short the pockets peeked out.

"Rosemary!" my parents snapped.

"Frances Shmances," Rosemary said. "Stop staring at me." She'd always wanted me on her side, before. As quick as her little file darted I'd become the enemy, too.

Uncle Bill, Aunt Emily, and our cousin Tricia stood waiting outside the locked cabin when we pulled in. Keys in hand, my mother hopped out of the car and ran to the front door. I stood for a second next to the car, hearing the ticking of the cooling engine. The smell of the lake drifted up, encircling us all, and for a second, I felt what I was waiting to feel: A wholeness, as if in unison, we would strip down to our playful selves as we did every summer. The selves that swam naked in the dark water. Watched sparks from the campfire spit up into the night sky. Laughed with each other instead of sniped at each other.

Rosemary slammed the car door and snatched her suitcase from the back of the car.

"Where did Charlie go off to already?" my mother said, swiveling around to see where my father had gone.

"You know how he likes to drag that boat out first thing," Aunt Emily said, shifting her armload of grocery bags. "Bill, go help Charlie." My mom gave Aunt Em a little smile. My mom was a younger sister, too.

I looked around. Where had Rosemary and Tricia gone off to so fast?

Forget them, I thought, and nosed in right behind my mother. I loved the smell of the cabin, damp, earthy, summery. The house had wide planked floors, shelves stacked with thousand piece puzzles, shoe boxes full of poker chips, incomplete card decks, and piles of musty romance novels. Kerosene lamps dotted tables and hung over chairs; there was no electricity. I loved the soft whooshing sound the lamps made when lit. Down a short path in the woods sat the outhouse, ripe and piney smelling.

I helped my mother lift up and secure the large wooden shutters, and sunlight shot through the windows. I peered out and glimpsed Tricia and Rosemary, standing knee deep in the still, green water. I could also see Sassafras Island; Rosemary and my father both liked to swim out to it, but it was too far for me, and I had never liked the dark bottomless part of the lake. Sassafras reminded me of old-fashioned ladies' bathing caps—rising bulbous and dense from the water with outcroppings of various trees and shrubs. On the other side of the lake was Camp Randolph, whose slogan was *To Make Good Boys Better*. In the light streaming in, dust motes floated on the air currents pulsing off the lake. I pushed open the screen door to the back porch and plopped down on a rocking chair, picking at the threads on my cut-offs. Rosemary and Tricia weren't standing in the water anymore. Where had they gone?

Through an open window in the kitchen, I heard my mother and Aunt Emily opening the old fridge which ran off a generator. They were tucking away the milk and hotdogs, the slabs of cheese and the loaves of banana bread with chocolate chips I'd helped my mom make the day before. In the cupboards, they stashed bags of chips, crackers, and boxes of raisins we'd packed up that morning.

"Tell me now while everyone's out of the house," Aunt Em said, her voice low.

I stopped rocking.

"We're piecing things back together, I think."

While I listened, my father and Uncle Bill emerged from around the cabin, dragging the heavy rowboat toward the water. I hoped they wouldn't spot me and call hello.

"Well, I think Charlie seems glad to be here," my Aunt Em said.

I could hear the patter of my mom's flip flops as she walked around the kitchen. "It's not too early for a gin and tonic, is it?"

"I've got the limes in my hand already," Aunt Em said.

The boat was at the water's edge. I was afraid to move.

"Oh look, they got the old behemoth out," my mom cried. The sharp scent of limes drifted to me.

"Frances!" I'd been spotted by my mother. Her head poked out the window. "How long have you been sitting there? Where are the other girls?"

"I can't find them anywhere." And, as if my little lie had come true, when I got up and started shouting their names, no one answered.

When Aunt Em gonged the dinner bell, Rosemary and Tricia barreled in, the screen door slapping behind them.

"Where'd you guys go?" I asked, setting down a plate of sliced tomatoes on the table in the screened porch facing the lake.

"We snuck around to spy on the boys' camp!" Tricia said.

"Shh. Don't tell," Rosemary clucked. She slid into a chair and put her elbows on the table and her chin on her fists. "We ran for nothing. Where is everyone?"

"You could help already," I said, sitting down across from her.

"I'll go get us milk," Tricia said.

After Tricia left the porch, Rosemary whispered to me, "Hasn't she gotten chubby this year?"

Uncle Bill and my father had already been fishing and came onto the porch with grilled trout. Aunt Em carried in the platter of steaming corn-on-the-cob. My mother squeezed my shoulder as she sat down next to me. Before we ate, Uncle Bill asked us all to say something for which we were thankful. He nodded at my mom.

"Me?" my mother said. "Family. My lovely family."

"Amen," Aunt Em said and reached a hand across the table and touched my mother's hand.

Uncle Bill turned to my father. My father wore a short sleeve, blue and white striped button-down shirt. The gold watch he wore to the office was still on his wrist, instead of the battered Timex that came out on weekends and vacations. He looked like a visitor. I felt vaguely sick and like I was going to cry. Maybe I was going to get my very first period. Not here with the outhouse, I prayed.

"Of course I'm thankful for my three wonderful children and— lovely wife—"

Rosemary said, under her breath, "Gag me."

I could hear the wind blowing in the trees. My mother swirled the ice cubes in her empty glass.

The beeswax candle flames dipped toward me in the breeze and my mother whispered softly, "Frances?"

"I'm thankful that Uncle Bill caught this fish, because it looks so good, but I hope they didn't feel any pain because we're all living creatures." I'd write a poem about that later. Living creatures. Sustaining each other. I needed some rhymes too.

"Jesus! They're only fish!" Rosemary said with a snort. She was wearing a bright green halter top and her shoulders were golden in the light.

"Shhh! Nice, Frances," my mother said. "Your turn, Rosemary."

"I don't play stupid games anymore. I'm only here because you made me come. Feel free to ignore me." Her green eyes were bright and challenging. We all looked at her as she reached forward and served herself up a big helping of the trout. "The best fish is a dead fish," she said. The candle flames wavered as my eyes filled with tears. I stared at my plate and concentrated on picking through each morsel, carefully sorting out the needle-like bones from the flesh.

Rosemary ate ferociously and then excused herself. She slammed through the door from the screened porch to the porch with the rockers and the hammock. She just stood there, looking out at the water. She looked a little tragic, and I almost felt sorry for her. My father speared a tomato with his fork and announced loudly that nothing had ever tasted better. My mother, chewing very slowly, stared out through the screen at Rosemary. "Good fish," remarked my aunt to my uncle.

From some skimpy fold in her short cut-offs, Rosemary produced a cigarette, as if this was something she did every day. My mother pushed back from the table and darted outside.

"Rosemary!" my mother shouted and stood with her fists on her hips. "A smart beautiful girl like you, smoking! Put it out."

Rosemary raised her eyebrows and looked at our mother.

"Whatever you say, mother." She dropped the cigarette in the short grass and stooped down to pound it out with a rock. "Nasty cigarette." She glared at my mother. "You're right. What was I thinking? I'm so glad you're here to make sure my life stays on track. You're doing such a good job with yours, by the way." She pounded the cigarette a few more times.

"Nasty, nasty, NASTY." My father threw down his fork and flashed out the door.

"Don't talk that way to your mother, Rosemary," he said, his voice firm and loud. His fisted hands were on his hips.

Rosemary stood up, rock in hand, and stared at him.

"You two are so dense. Asinine. Pathetic." She dropped the rock on the porch next to my mother's bare feet and walked away. My mother's hands unclenched and dropped limply to her sides. My father put his arm around her, and they stood like that, awkward.

I pushed back from the table so quickly my water almost spilled. "Let's play Hearts after dinner! I'll find the cards. Tricia? Anyone?"

Everyone just watched as Rosemary stalked off down the dock, shedding her clothes down to her underwear as she went. She jumped then and seemed to float weightless for a split second on a warm cushion of night air before she dropped from view into the jade-dark water.

That night as we lay in bed, I heard the moths butting against the screens and the slow swoosh of water against the dock. Tricia snored lightly.

"Rosemary," I said.

"Hmm?"

"Do you think Mom and Dad are going to be ok? Stay together?" I could barely say it, the words hurting my throat.

"Let me look in my crystal ball..." she said in the wavery witchy voice she used when we played with the Ouija board. "Don't worry about it, okay? There's nothing we can do about it."

"Today I felt like I might get my period."

"Lucky you. Write a poem about it."

My father woke me at dawn.

His hand patted my shoulder. "Wanna go fishing?" he whispered.

Our summer ritual. I carried his mug of coffee down to the boat, while he loaded in the tackle and rods. The house behind us was dark and quiet. The oars in the gunwales clanked softly, and the smell of the blades, like moist soil, wafted in the cool air. I sipped Dad's coffee and pulled my hood up over my head.

He rowed us for a while until the light on top of the ruffled water turned pink.

"This spot looks promising," he said and pulled the oars in. We set to work. I didn't mind putting the worms on the hook. I didn't want to be a fake. If I ate the fish, I should be okay with catching the fish. If I fished, I shouldn't get squeamish about the worm. My dad flung his line way out, and I dropped mine straight on down. I wondered how far down it was to the bottom.

We fished in silence. I had always thought it was so that we wouldn't alert the fish to our presence. I had always enjoyed the hush that magnified the sounds of water splishing when we dropped in our lines, the birds beginning to sing, the far away sounds of life from the boys' camp. This year though, looking at my father's profile, watching his eyes scan the water, I thought, what is he thinking? What does he want? It made my stomach hurt.

Eventually, a fish nibbled my line, but when I reeled it in, he'd made off with the worm. My father caught two trout in succession and put them in our cooler. When the smells of breakfast from the boys' camp skimmed over the water toward us, we both agreed it was time to row home. When the sun came up, the magic was gone for me.

"Frances, why don't you take the seat of honor here?" my dad said and rose up. As he held on to the sides of the boat, I ducked under his arm and sat down in the exact middle of the seat. My hands still barely fit around the oars' grips. I put my back toward the bow, toward home. Facing my father and his hopeful grinning face, I rowed.

We zigzagged a bit since I couldn't coordinate the oars, nor barely lift them off the top of the water without a little lunge of my arms. What if an oar slipped out and sank down to the bottom of the lake? Sweat itched my scalp and my hands began to ache, but we'd barely gone anywhere. A burning sensation between my shoulder blades made me wonder if I'd pulled a muscle. I stopped and pulled the oars in.

"Dad."

"Done? Nice try. Next year you'll be rowing like a pro. I just know it," my father said. "At least this way I know you'll still be my fishing partner."

I was sure that he was disappointed in me. But he had said, 'next year.'

We carefully switched places. As he rowed home, I noticed he was wearing his Timex. I tucked my chin and pretended to be fascinated by a small cut on my finger as tears rolled down my nose.

"What's up there, Frana Banana?"

"Don't know." I wiped my nose with the back of my hand and felt embarrassed and glad he'd noticed. He'd stopped rowing and put his elbows on his knees, the oars held loosely.

"Things aren't always as much fun as they look from far away, I guess," I said. "And Rosemary is being a B-I-T-"

"I see your point."

"Mom says that Rosemary is going through things, how a cater-pillar changes into a butterfly but how they go deep into themselves first. She says be patient."

The sun edged up behind the early morning haze ringing the lake. It was very still.

"Your mom is usually right, Frances," my dad said and wiped a tear on the edge of my nose with a knuckle.

After breakfast, Rosemary, Tricia, and I walked to our sunbathing spot, on an old weather-silvered dock reached by a leafy path that edged the lake. We spread out our towels and laid out our supplies: baby oil, chips, cold water, Lip Smackers, back issues of *Seventeen* magazines, and a novel, *The Godfather*, which Tricia had found on a shelf in the house. I stared at the fullness that popped out of Tricia and Rosemary's bikini tops when they untied the strings. These were not my mother's tube sock breasts. I thought about my own little nubbins and willed them to bloom.

Rosemary pulled a gold and green Miller out her bag and snapped it open.

"Where'd you get that?"

"Where do you think, Frances?"

"You're not supposed to be drinking beer."

"Want a sip, Tricia? Don't be such a baby, Frances." Rosemary was lying on her stomach. She swigged the beer and pushed it toward Tricia.

Our skin glistened with baby oil and Tricia found some sex scenes in *The Godfather* that she read out-loud. Then, from over the still green lid of the lake came the clunking sound of a paddle against an aluminum canoe.

"Boys!" I shouted and sat up straighter with my towel pressed to my chest.

"About time." Rosemary flipped a page of *Seventeen*, but her eyes were up, scanning, damp red curls against her shoulders which were turning pink.

"Cover up, you guys!" I shouted. A canoe on the right side of the lake edged its way in our direction. Its silvery body reflected the smooth lake surface. I could see the painted green and black wildcat eyes on either side of the bow and the two long-armed teen boys in it. A Camp Randolph canoe. Tricia continued to lie on her stomach, but she reached under herself to pull up her bikini top and then she asked me to tie it around her neck, which I did, quickly, in a double knot.

Rosemary dipped her fingers over the edge of the dock and ran them across her brow and between her breasts. Her chest was starting to look red and splotchy from the heat.

"Rosemary, *come on.* Cover up!"

"Chill out, Francy Pants. They can't see us from way over there." Still lying on her stomach, she arched her back to get a better view of the lake. "And so what? Who here is tired of playing Hearts at night with our parents? I sure as hell am." Her brown freckles stood out on her pink face.

"Rosemary! They'll see your boobs."

"Good. I don't even care."

"Oh, I think you care," Tricia said, "I think you care quite a bit, Rosemary." Tricia crossed her tan plumpish legs and pulled a bottle of Summer Peach nail polish out of her swimming bag. She shook it so the metal ball inside made tiny clacking noises, and then she unscrewed it and carefully began painting her fingernails.

Rosemary flipped on her back and her pink breasts flattened. "You guys have no sense of adventure." She put her hands behind her neck and began to do sit-ups. She jackknifed her legs up and over until her toes touched the dock behind her red curls, which fanned out around her, like a crown of fire.

The canoe was sliding through the water, heading straight toward us, slicing the lake in two. Then the boat began to fishtail, as if the boys were trying to outdo each other. I remembered one of Newton's laws of motion from science class. *An object in motion continues in motion with the same speed and in the same direction unless acted upon by an unbalanced force.* The distance between them and us was quickly swallowed. I followed each stroke, hoping hoping hoping they'd veer off in some other direction. Tricia watched them over her nails. Rosemary continued her stretching. I threw my towel at her and she batted it away.

Then they were there at our dock. The boy in the bow was long-armed and broad-shouldered and needed a shave. The boy in the stern was shirtless and wore a Red Sox hat. I thought his chest looked lovely and warm, but a little pimply. They looked like counselors, not campers.

"It must be August. The girls are back," said the tall one in the bow, doing a little twist with his paddle in the water to stop the unsteady canoe.

"We sent those campers on a scavenger hunt they'll never finish, so we could go bird watching!" They both thought this was hilarious. The boat rocked softly near the dock. I could smell sweat and peanut butter sandwiches and suntan lotion. Two crushed Pabst cans sat among some beers that rolled around bottom of the boat.

Rosemary sat up, cupping her hands over her breasts. The soles of her feet faced the boys.

"*Go away*, why don't you." I pointed in the direction of the house. "Our parents are just over there."

"Frances!" Tricia and Rosemary both shushed me.

I glared at Tricia.

"Girls who sunbathe in the raw get burned," the tall one said. He had a pair of binoculars in his lap. Both boys had a hand on the dock now. "Tie this will you?" Rosemary said and looked at me, eyebrow raised, chin up in a challenge. She crossed her legs, Indian style. She dropped her cupped hands for a second and slowly pulled up her bikini top. I yanked the strings until she said, "Ow!" The boys were disgusting, practically drooling like our stupid dog when it treed a cat.

"You girls want a beer?" Red Sox held one out.

"Got our own," Rosemary tipped back what was left of the Miller.

Tricia carefully applied polish to her toes now, not catching my eye.

"Have you girls ever been to that little island?" Bow man pointed toward Sassafras.

"Never!" Rosemary declared.

"What?! You swim to it every summer and take the boat there sometimes!"

"Don't butt in," Rosemary shushed me. "Don't mind her," she said and rolled her eyes at the boys. I wanted to slap her.

"So who wants to go then? You?" Bow man said and pointed at Rosemary. "You?" He pointed at Tricia. "You?" He gave me a disgusting grin.

I stood up and grabbed my towel and bag. "You guys. Let's. Go. Home."

Rosemary looked flushed and fiery, and I wanted to kick her into the water. She slipped her big white t-shirt on over her pink shoulders. Tricia screwed the nail polish top on the bottle and slipped it into her straw beach bag. Was she with Rosemary, or me?

Rosemary hopped to her feet.

"Give me a hand, will you?" She reached out for Red Sox's hand, then stepped so one foot was on the weathered dock and one foot was on the wobbling bottom of the aluminum canoe, so blinding in the sun. The boat started to drift. Rosemary held herself there, poised for a second between boat and dock and turned her head to look at me. "I'll be back, Frances. Don't worry."

But I did worry. My mind was taken up with thoughts of worry for her, but an image of me kept pushing up through the chaos. Me. Alone. Forever diminished by Rosemary's acts of boldness. I wasn't afraid for her at all. The boys looked a little surprised, too, to find her right there between them. Rosemary grabbed the paddle from the one in the stern, settled herself in the middle and said, "Let's go!" biting her paddle into the water with force. Look at her! I thought, almost proud for a moment. I watched her lean forward, rowing on this side and then that side as the canoe skittered away into the hollow dark of the lake.

Tricia and I watched the silvery canoe edge around the lake, away from the house, cut through the middle to Sassafras Island, and disappear into the greenery that draped the dark water.

Quickly, I gathered my things, shaking out my towel in search of my flip-flops.

"Chill out," Tricia said, "She's just going for a canoe ride to the island."

"We don't know those boys!"

"God, don't have a cow already! Sit down." Panic rose up in me with the taste of that morning's bacon and eggs. My palm went cold and sweaty. What were they planning to *do* to her? I walked around and around the small dock. I coughed and took a drink from my water bottle.

"What do you think is going on?" I asked.

Tricia grabbed a handful of chips and stuffed them in her mouth.

"*Tricia*," I said. "I should run home and tell my mom and dad. Don't you think?"

"Lie down, Frances. You're making me nervous."

Nothing moved near the island.

I spread my towel out and lay down on my stomach, pressing my eye to a space in the dock like a gap in teeth. It was dark down there, but I could hear the lapping of the water against the pilings and smell rotting wood. Rosemary was reckless. I thought about the golden colored chest of the one boy.

When I turned my head to the side, I could see the end of the long dock that jutted out from the house. My father was there now, down on one knee, next to the cooler of fish. But his back was to the lake, his head bowed. He wouldn't have seen anything. The canoe stayed out of sight. The island remained secretive. Only a few minutes had passed, but the knots in my gut felt like they'd been there forever.

"Frances!" Tricia yelped jumping up, her hand above her eyes like a salute.

We saw a canoe glide away from the island toward the boys' camp, but the middle seat was empty. I jumped up and down trying to get a better angle. What I saw was what I always saw. A crater filled with dark water. Wide flat lily pads at the edges. Sparkles of sun like rolling marbles on the lake's surface, a beautiful lid over the blackness.

A wind had kicked up, and the lake looked restless and skittish. The boys never turned their heads our way.

"Oh my God, what have they done with her?" I pushed my feet into my yellow flip-flops and began to run, leaving Tricia behind as still as a statue.

The scrubby pines and maples and sassafras lining the path scratched at my legs and their scent stung my nostrils as I sped back toward the house. It was hotter there, off the water, and I was breath-less and sweaty. I passed the screen porch, where my mother and Aunt Emily sat with coffee cups and magazines. Uncle Bill snoozed in the hammock with a book on his belly. I ran past them all toward the dock.

My father was still on one knee. His head was tucked low, a silver-bellied trout in one hand and a knife in the other. He drove the knife into the underbelly of the fish and pulled it down toward the tail. Blood oozed out and down his hand. He reached inside the fish and pulled out the entrails. I'd never seen my father gut a fish. That was Uncle Bill's pleasure, and my father left it to him. But here he was, my father, in the hot sun, before our catch. I stood there staring.

"Where's the fire, Frances?"

"Rosemary went out in a canoe with some boys, and they left her on Sassafras! They paddled away without her!" I gestured to the island.

He stood up, hands gooey and red. "What?" He turned his head toward the island and now we saw her, a white speck in her T-shirt. My mother, who saw me flash by, stood on the dock behind me, her hand at her brow, staring out at the island. At the speck that was Rosemary.

"What? Boys? Left her there?" she said. "Rosemary!" she yelled.

"Slow down everybody. Just slow down." My dad knelt at the edge of the dock and swished his hands quickly in the water.

"I told her not to!" I said, knowing I should have run home the second Rosemary had started preening. "I told them all you were right over here!" My mother ran to unhitch the boat.

"If anything happened over there," my dad said and clenched his wet fists, keeping his eye on Rosemary. His voice was a low growl I'd never heard.

My mother handed the rope from the boat to my father.

"Why is she doing this to me?" she said.

"It's not always about you, Anita," my father spluttered, jackknif-ing his body into the boat.

My mother's gray eyes looked fuzzy with tears. "Do you think she's okay?" She locked her eyes on Rosemary as if watchfulness could carry my sister home.

All of us had gathered on the dock now. We watched as my dad's arms and the oars were like one, widening into a great V. He gathered strength and speed, leaving little whirlpools in his wake.

I watched hard, my toes curled over the edge of the dock, my arms wrapped around me. I didn't want to look at my mother. I could hear her breathing hard, as if she were rowing the boat. It looked like Rosemary was standing up now, hands on her hips, waiting. My father was looking over his shoulder, bee-lining it. *Please everyone be okay.* Tears made my nose sting, and the smell of fish and blood made me feel like throwing up.

My father reached the island. I saw the white speck of Rosemary move into the boat. My father turned the boat around, bow toward home.

In the middle of the slate color water that separated the dock from the island, they stopped. Rosemary got up and ducked under my father's arm as he steadied the boat, just as I had done that morning. She held the shiny smooth oar handles, stretched forward with arms winged out and caught the water. I knew how heavy the oars were, how they had minds of their own. I could see power gather in the muscles between Rosemary's shoulder blades, each stroke becoming stronger and more sure.

As if a hand pushed my back, as if my own will had nothing to do with it, I plunged into the green water and began to swim as I heard my mother calling, "Frances!"

I swam furiously, my muscles hot with the effort. My skin tingled from water that grew colder as I went farther, as the water got deeper.

I stopped for a moment and treaded water, swirling my hands to turn myself and see where I was. My mother on the dock was not as far as I had thought. Imagined or real fish slipped against my legs. My mother's calls rippled toward me, across the water.

I envisioned the hand that had pushed me off that dock now holding the top of my head, keeping me in place. My lungs were so tight and hot I worried they'd pop. I thought of Rosemary, poised over the water, weightless, unafraid.

I tried to swim on with my eyes closed and my legs furiously scissoring the lake's sheen. My belly began to cramp. My shoulders ached. There was gaping nothingness below and all around.

Then my father was there, dragging me into the rowboat, covering me with his t-shirt.

I shivered, crouching in the bottom of the boat, sucking in the air. I didn't dare look at Rosemary or my father as my father took the oars.

When we got back to the dock, my mother reached for me and wrapped me in a huge striped towel and murmured tender and pity-ing words in my ear. I heard my father whisper, "They're both fine."

To Rosemary, who stepped out of the boat smug and haughty, my mother said, "We'll talk about this later, young lady." I wrenched away from my mother's arms, cold and exhausted, and ran down the dock.

I locked the door of our room, took my suit off, and lay under the blankets of my bed. Rosemary pounded on the door.

"Let me in. I need some clothes for God's sake." When I didn't answer she said, "Don't take it personally, Frances. Come on now."

I unlocked the door but didn't open it and dove back under my blankets. For a while, she rustled around and then left, shutting the door quietly.

As dusk fell, I grew hungry, starving, and came downstairs. My father and mother were side by side on the screen porch, leaning over a crossword puzzle on the table. Uncle Bill and Aunt Emily had taken Rosemary and Tricia into town to see the late movie. The grill was still hot and my dad put a burger on for me while my mother searched the fridge for bleu cheese to crumble on it, just how I liked it. They sat on one side of the table, and I sat on the other as I ate.

"You worked up an appetite today," my dad said.

"Rosemary said to tell you sorry she didn't listen to you," my mom said and reached across the table and patted my hand. "I think her exact words were, 'I'm such an idiot. I should have listened to Fran-ces,'" my dad added.

"Well, she is an idiot." I took a large mouthful of burger and felt the bite of the bleu cheese against my tongue.

"We all do stupid things. Rash things. Things we're sorry for." My dad's voice was low.

The candles flickered in the warm August breeze rattling the screens.

"I'm full," I said, standing up with my plate.

"How about a game of Hearts," my mom suggested. "The three of us?"

"No," I said. "I'm just going to go read in bed."

Up in my room, I pulled out a pad of paper to try to write a poem, but I couldn't make any sense out of the jumble of emotions inside me. It was all flashing images that wouldn't slow down enough for me to catch them. I must have fallen asleep. When I awoke later, it was dark and I could make out the lumps of Rosemary and Tricia under their sheets.

From the open window, I heard the squeak of the screen door.

"Hey, are you coming to bed?" My mother's voice floated softly up on the humid night air.

"I must have fallen asleep. Come here," my father said. I heard the porch creak and the slap of my mother's flip-flops. They made the sounds of two bodies arranging themselves.

"What a day, huh?" My father's voice.

"Did you see Frances jump in? If I wasn't so scared for her, I would have laughed," my mother said, her voice was full of love. "Rosemary. What are we going to do with her?"

"I guess she's doing what she's supposed to be doing. What teens do," my father said.

It was quiet for a moment, save the slow swinging sound of the hammock.

"And sometimes grown men."

"Touché."

I pressed my ear to the screen.

"You have a bug on your arm," my mother said, and I heard the sound of a small slap.

"Got it?"

"I don't know." Her voice was gone, and it came out a slow sob. And the sound of light slaps, over and over, came through the screen, and I pictured her capable hands raining down on him. I could hear her crying.

Rosemary turned over and sighed in her sleep.

"Hey," my father said, soft and low, "hey, hey sweetie." And the slaps stopped like he'd caught her wrists in his hands.

"It hurts," my mother said.

"Does it hurt here? Or here?" Whatever my father was doing was twisting my mother's cries into laughs and the hammock slowed. And I could hear their breathing like a wind, circling up and catching us in it.

The Sari

The clanking of metal invaded Sarah's dream in which her mother, dressed in a silky robe, knelt in front of a kitchen cabinet searching for a pot to boil eggs. "Oh my God, I can't find anything around here anymore," she said and began pulling out strands of her graying golden hair.

Sarah woke and felt her face for tears, but her face was dry. She pressed her fingers around her body for lumps or pain, but there was none. She felt emptied. The sound was Chandra clanking a pot in the courtyard at the water spigot. The rhesus monkeys screamed and hurled nuts on the metal roof overhead. Sarah was thousands of miles from Boston, in Ahmedabad, India. Her mother wasn't there, or anywhere, anymore.

Sarah looked at Lisa asleep in the bed against the other wall. Four rooms opened out onto a large, unroofed courtyard, two American students in each room. Sarah slipped on her loose cotton pants and tunic, eyeing Lisa's blue and gold sari folded neatly on the shelf. Sarah touched the edge of the sari, remembering the day Lisa bought it. One of their first days in India, they'd been returning in a rickshaw from a bank where they'd spent over an hour changing money. Lisa had spotted the tailor's shop and called to the rickshaw driver to stop. She went inside while Sarah waited, leaning against the building, looking at her toes rimmed in red dust and choking in the mid-day mugginess. A young man in black pants and a tight maroon shirt nudged her. Did she know his uncle in Chicago? The tailor poked her head out the door, "Come in! Have a look!" Sarah heard Lisa laughing from inside the shop, enjoying her transformation at the hands of this woman.

To take such delight. To be transformed. It seemed foreign to Sarah then and still did.

   Sarah wore the cotton cloth woven by the students. It was the color of oatmeal and coarse against her skin. Every morning, all the Indian students at the Vidyapith went to the great hall to sit in neat rows and hand spin cotton and sing morning prayers. Gandhi believed in the principle of self-sufficiency. The American exchange students made lumpy string that could not be used for anything.

   Sarah slipped on her sandals and quietly left the room. The burn of yesterday's dhal and potato curry gripped Sarah's bowels. She crossed the courtyard to the toilet stall, a hole in the ground. After squatting, she flushed with a pail of water and washed her hands at the water spigot.

   A blue light came from the small kitchen. She could hear the whoosh of the gas stove and knew Chandra was making their tea and breakfast chapattis.

   Cross-legged in the middle of the courtyard, Sarah waited for the others. The chameleon sky took on the colors of the land below it, green like the Sabarmati River, rust like the dust that coated everything, blue-white like the flames of stoves that burned throughout the city. Sarah closed her eyes and tried to pay attention to her breathing like the yogi showed them at a meditation class the students attended, an attempt to understand Indian culture and religion.

   Roger, long-haired and loose-limbed, emerged from his room. He rubbed Sarah's neck and she felt his big thumbs on the muscles around her shoulder blades. He breathed in her ear, "Om mani padme hum."

   "Hi." She hadn't been able to meditate anyway. Sometimes she felt like her mind was like a box with a jigsaw puzzle in it in a thousand pieces. Everything was there, but she couldn't figure it out. She felt vague, without edges, not sure about anything.

   "Did you hear the fireworks last night?" Roger asked. It was Diwali, the five day festival of lights.

   "I actually slept through it," Sarah admitted, though she didn't tell him she took something to help her sleep. Roger worried; she felt like his project. On the flight from Boston to India the group sat together toward the back of the plane and became acquainted. Sarah had felt uneasy about leaving her father, but hadn't wanted to stay. She didn't want to go back to Middlebury, to her gaggle of kind friends who hadn't a clue what it felt like to lose a mother. But she'd walked reluctantly onto the plane that would take her thousands of miles from everything familiar. On the plane, the other American exchange students had read guide books, practiced Gujarati, ordered little bottles of liquor and tucked them in their carry-on bags. Roger had seemed like a sensitive animal, sniffing out what was missing or what used to be there. He found her a pillow and a blanket and saved her food, which was delivered while she slept.

"Wanna run today?" he asked her now.

"I'm going to meet the sweepers." Her independent study project. One of their guides around the city had pointed out sweepers everywhere, bent over their little brooms. They were forming a cooperative, the guide told them, getting their women's rights!

Roger picked up her hand and traced its bones with his fingers.

"Let's meet back here this afternoon. One o'clockish?" He had green eyes that wanted to know her and the long arms and tight torso of the rower he had been back at Brown. The first time they'd slept together was when the others went on a field trip to a local village. She lay in her bed while he told the guide they both had diarrhea and couldn't ride the bus that far.

"I'll see." If she'd met him a year ago, his strong hands and bright eyes would have filled her with eagerness and silliness.

"I might do errands after my meeting." Buy eggs maybe, she thought; the rust colored dhal they ate at every meal filled her with longings.

"Oh." Roger dropped her hand. She was hot and cold with him and she knew it and couldn't help it. Her stomach hurt again and she didn't know if it was related to the food or if was from the little punch in the stomach she felt when he let go of her.

"I might buy eggs," she said, trying to reconnect. "I'll boil some for you." And we can eat them later, she thought, still steaming and sprinkled with salt out of our hands. Her mother had a prized collection of little porcelain egg cups that looked like dancing women.

Ramesh, her advisor, came on his red scooter to take her to meet the sweeper women. Sitting behind him, she had to hold his soft middle to keep from being lurched off the bike as he swerved through streets thick with rickshaws, cows, people hauling carts, trucks belching diesel exhaust.

Ramesh put a toe on the ground and paused as a funeral procession snaked across the street and down toward the Sabarmati. They were in the square with the bronze statue of Gandhi. Drums beat and people wailed. A child picked up stones and tried to juggle. Sarah closed her eyes as the body on a bamboo pallet bumped and jostled by.

They had tossed her mother's ashes into the Atlantic from the beach at Race Point. It had been a windy May day. Their brightly colored foul weather gear caught the bone dust the gusting wind brought back. It coated her like the fine mist spraying off the waves. A man walking his golden retriever had stopped and watched. Sarah had been unable to help noticing his drooling dog growling at a stick, front legs down, rear up, wanting to play. She hated that he distracted her, that later that day she could remember more of him than of the ceremony for her mother.

As the scooter idled, a plump woman came out of a whitewashed shop. The woman was the tailor Lisa had dragged Sarah to. Her smooth skin shone like polished copper and she looked like autumn, in a crimson sari flecked with gold, with a red tika in the middle of her forehead. The woman laughed after she and Ramesh exchanged some words.

"American girl again she says! Dressed like a peasant Indian man. She thinks you look funny. See the sign? She's a tailor." Ramesh chuckled.

The heat and dust and traffic smells made her want to throw up. Glancing back as the scooter roared to life, she saw the woman, red-gold in the ray of sun, glass bangles on her wrist shimmering as she waved goodbye.

When they arrived at the Ahmedabad Technical College where the sweepers worked, Sarah's hair was wind-blown, her skin covered by a fine net of dust and sweat. Ramesh's black hair looked neat as a book of matches and his silk shirt was sweatless.

Ramesh called to the women. Then he was gone in a wave of the scent of after-shave. Sarah felt like she was standing in front of a group of hungry squirrels. The women squatted and pulled the ends of their faded cotton saris over their heads, their twiggy feet poking out. They twisted arm bangles, picked at their teeth with pieces of straw, pulled at the loops of gold in their ears.

"Namaste," Sarah said, her mouth dry. They were pleased and chatted among themselves; Sarah felt dizzy in the thick buzz of the foreign language.

A woman in a maroon sari walked over and plucked at Sarah's pants. Sarah's stomach gurgled and burned. Another woman put her fingers in Sarah's thick, straight hair. A smooth, papery palm ran down her arm. Sarah stared into the empty cup of her hands and felt her body stiffen and shrink. A pearl of sweat rolled between her shoulder blades. Hands were all over her body. Her mother used to come behind her and put her hands in Sarah's jeans pocket. What does it feel like to be you? she'd say. Sarah wanted to sink into the floor, melt away.

Sarah lay on her bed with the wooden shutters closed. The smell of rotten bananas filled the room. She would bring her own pillow if she ever came to India again. And brush up on her folk songs. Wherever they went, people asked them to sing. She couldn't even carry a tune.

Roger opened the door before she could say come in. The sun from the courtyard was at his back, his face a blur. He moved toward her with open hands and face. He held onto her ribs and kissed her shoulders. She willed herself to focus. To feel. He looked small and far away. Her skin felt numb. She pictured the dead bodies burning.

His rough cheek burned her face. Tears filled the curved shells of her ears. Her mother had lost her diamond solitaire three times. Once in the snow by the mailbox. A neighbor had seen it sparkle the following spring. The second time her mother had remembered last seeing it when she was mashing potatoes. She'd helped her mother search everywhere, closets, kitchen drawers, the insides of pants pockets and her tan leather gloves. The diamond had fallen to the floor when Sarah had pulled out the Boston Yellow Pages. The third time the stone had come loose from the prongs; her father had said he'd get it set with six prongs if they found it. Her mother had said, "There isn't time this time!" Her voice all sharp edges where it had once been smooth, like sea-washed stones.

Roger rose up on his elbows. He dotted Sarah's wet face with kisses.

"You're awesome," he said. But Sarah was spinning in a black space he mistook for joy or didn't notice at all. The emptiness inside of her filled with pity for his being so clueless, and disgust at herself for letting him stay that way. She wanted a scalding hot shower. But she couldn't even get a bucket of cold water because they only had water between 6 and 9 a.m. and 5 and 7 p.m.

Lisa came back from a lesson on the Bharatanatyam moving her hands and fingers in graceful twisting ways.

"Girls spend ten years learning the dance, Sarah." Lisa tried to move her neck from side to side while keeping her head completely level. "It takes two years just to learn the hand movements, and every little move has a specific meaning." Lisa snapped on an ankle bracelet with bells.

"But why?" Sarah pulled her sheet tighter so Lisa wouldn't see she was naked.

"Why what?"

"I don't understand the point of spending ten years on a dance?"

"Why'd you come to India, anyway?" Lisa said, gently, as she ran a hand through her short blonde hair. Her sari was coming untucked at the waist, showing her plumpness, the Indian ideal of beauty. When Sarah didn't answer, Lisa picked up the Bhagavad Gita she was reading and went into the courtyard. A second later, she stuck her arm back in.

"Mail."

Sarah took the thick manila envelope covered with stamps and her father's lefty scrawl from Lisa. She held it in her hands and opened it slowly. The air that escaped the envelope smelled like her mother's stationary drawer, pencil shavings and lilac scented paper. Her mother would have typed long, newsy letters; a review of the current novel she was reading, a lambaste of local politics and how conservative the town was growing, sightings from the fall birdfeeder, designs for her new scrap metal sculpture. Sarah dumped out the envelope and pieces of paper fluttered to her bed. There was a yellow sticky note. *Thought you might find the enclosed interesting. Muddling along without you. Lots of hugs and kisses. Dad.*

Clippings from the *Town Crier* about the Weston Wildcats field hockey team, for which she'd been captain her senior year. A recipe on how to make simple herbed chicken for one in a packet of foil. Sarah wondered if this enclosure was a mistake, revealing the chaos on her father's desk. Finally, the Order of Service from the Unitarian Church on October 15, with a photo clipped on. Her father had circled one of the announcements in royal blue pen.

"The flowers on the altar this morning are given in the loving memory of Jennifer S. Dixon, by her devoted husband and loving daughter, Edward J. Dixon and Sarah C. Dixon."

The picture showed the arrangement of flowers set against the dark wood at the front of the church. Yellow freesia, purple irises, white snapdragons, orange Chinese lanterns. Her mother's favorite flowers. The church announcements had been something for Sarah to read, to doodle over when she had been bored in church. Now, she held the picture in her hand, stunned at how little was left of a life.

Sarah found tiny nail scissors in her travel bag. She took the photo, and carefully cut around the image of the flower arrangement, letting bits of the church drop to the floor. She snipped the adhesive part off a Band-Aid and taped the flowers to a clean page in her journal. She put her nose to it, wishing she could smell something besides old paper. Then she got out some pens and drew a garden with woods all around the bright flowers.

Sarah woke early when Lisa rolled over in her sleep and kicked two books to the floor, *My Experiments with Truth*, by Gandhi, and *The Wonder That Was India*, by A.L. Basham. Lisa's shelf displayed little brass figures of Hindu gods: Brahma the Creator, Vishnu the Sustainer, Shiva the Destroyer. Lisa embraced all of it with nonjudgmental goodwill.

Sarah had signed up to go to India before her mother had fallen sick. A junior semester abroad; it had sounded exotic and full of questions and answers. It had made Sarah feel serious, grown-up. She'd been on the phone to cancel when her mother walked in, her head in a scarf, her cheek bones carved. "Put that phone down right now." The voice she'd used when Sarah was younger and being disobedient. Her mother's face had been hard. "This is shattering my life plan. I won't let it mess up yours." As if she had power.

Wind banged the shutters, and Sarah heard the sound of the damp cloth snapping. The dhobi had come the evening before and hung their washed and wrung clothes on lines he strung up across the open space. Their white cotton pants. Lisa's saris. Roger and Kevin's lungis they wore instead of pajamas. Sarah lay listening; it sounded like kites snapping on the wind. Her mother had loved kites. The day she and her father and aunts had scattered the ashes at Race Point, they wrote little notes on scraps of paper and twisted them on the wind-taut strings, where they twirled skyward. Her dad had written, "Jen, my one true love, may God keep you safe until I can hold you again." One of the aunts wrote, "You always had to be first. Why?" Sarah wouldn't read hers. She'd let go of the kite and watched it whip up, snatched away, into gray.

Lisa snored softly. Sarah wished for such an oblivious sleep that ended in such an enthusiastic waking. Every morning felt the same color of gray. She put her hands on her breasts and felt for lumps or pain. Her grandmother had died the same way as her mother had. Maybe when she got back to the U.S., she'd look into just getting them cut off. Sarah looked at her watch. She had to meet again with the sweepers, the women who swept every corner of the city. She was daunted by their hard work. Mystified by their words. Intrigued by the cooperative they were forming to protect themselves and empower themselves. But, she didn't know how to connect with them. Their bodies—stooped over their short-handled brooms—were in endless motion and constant service to others' dirt, and they came back each day and did it again and sang while they worked. She felt trapped and desperate with longing. She wanted to peel herself away like she peeled the shells of eggs.

The morning stillness and quiet made Sarah want to scream, to drown out her own self. She could knock on Roger's door, and he'd go running with her but his chatter would irritate her. She had to get out, to breathe hard, to sweat, to surround herself with others than herself. Sarah got up and put on yesterday's cotton tunic and loose drawstring pants. In the courtyard, she clapped her hands to scatter the monkeys.

The morning was dim and sounds came to her muffled in the still air. A man sat by the side of the road, firing up a small stove and set-ting out glasses with a clink. She crossed the Nehru Bridge and hit a wall of smells: dung fires, hibiscus, excrement, cinnamon. Women with saris pulled over their heads clapped breakfast chapattis with smooth hands. People slept, curled together like baby chicks on beds pulled outside on the pavement. Flip-flops slapped as people moved by, wrapped in blankets against the early morning chill. A child with yellow eyes squatted in an empty patch of dirt. Daughters of a dhobi walked toward the river with armloads of clothes to beat in the slug-gish Sabarmati with little wooden paddles. Sarah heard the clink of their bracelets, the songs they sang.

She was running and not paying attention to the turns. A little prick of fear poked at her. But she welcomed it like she welcomed the alarm. There might be a crack somewhere inside of her.

Sarah heard the singing and drumming first. In this city of thou-sands, the sounds of death were familiar to her now, though it still sounded to her like a happy parade was behind her. She moved to the side of the road as drumming men and a disorganized crowd moved toward her. The body, carried on a bamboo pallet, was draped in bright cloth and covered with marigolds. What looked like party streamers, or strips of colored cloth, were tied to the bier, flapping in the warm, dusty breeze. The body would be taken to the river for the ritual cleansing and to the Ghats for burning. A brightness, a feeling of celebration along with sadness, rippled through Sarah.

A woman in a green sari, frayed on the end, glanced shyly at Sarah and yanked the hand of a toddler who was distracted by a chicken. When he cried, his mother hoisted him onto a hip, and Sarah could see the swell of another child in her belly. One of the older boys carrying the body combed his eyes over Sarah as if he'd never seen such a sight, his glance curious and non-threatening.

She found herself following them, at the fringes, as if she was going that way. Golden marigolds lay scattered on the roadway. A white sheet draped the body. Who was up there? Sarah wondered. An older woman wrapped in a big gray shawl was crying loudly and shaking her head back and forth. The woman stopped to pick a rock out of her sandal, glanced back at the others and her crying stopped, then resumed again.

Sarah hung back, shadowing the mourners as they wended their way from more prominent streets with sidewalks and shops to roads and then alleys becoming progressively more narrow and primitive. She felt as if she were going back in time.

Finally they arrived at a set of stone steps that led down to the water. Dawn was breaking, rippling the water with its pink light. The men and boys carrying the body set the pallet down on the bottom step. The wailing swelled. Sarah closed her eyes; the atonal vibrations moved through her like an electric current. She tried to conjure up her mother's face and let the songs of grief swaddle them both. But the face was broken up, a collage. The eyes from the picture of her holding baby Sarah, the thirsty lips of those last days, the hair how it looked after she walked the dog in the rain, the cheeks curled up in a mischievous smile, the eyebrows missing.

She hurt from the effort. The unfamiliar noises began to suffocate her, raked against her ears like angry bees. She trembled as if cold and felt the earth spinning her off balance. The breeze off the water was warm and ripe like decay. She opened her eyes to see the cloth being peeled away, an arm that was ghastly yellow and the skull of an old man. Sickness rose up in her throat, hot and choking, and the sheen of adventure and courage and strength blew away like ashes.

She turned and ran. The path went up, away from the river and then flattened, and she was lost in a maze of little alleyways. The ground was uneven, rutted by mangy dogs, holy skinny cows, and the bare feet of beggars. She ran. She turned right then left, guessing the direction. A prick of light from a cigarette glowed in the doorway of a tin shack. Sarah was afraid the man smoking it would reach out and grab her, yet she wanted to be grabbed. The world was like a spinning tea-cup, those stupid fair rides that made her sick. She only wanted to stop. Sarah heard the thumpity bump sound of the cart ahead of her. The man pulling it had his head down as he strained like an ox with his heavy load. They passed too close to one another, and Sarah caught her foot in the drainage ditch as she stepped to the side. She went down into the murk. Lurching to her feet she yelled after him, "Look up, Goddamn you!" He rumbled on, his head bent, whispering in rhythm with the wheels.

Her wet pants clung to her leg, the smell repulsive. Children defecated in those ditches. People would think she'd soiled herself. Saliva filled her mouth as if she would vomit. Sarah ran, looking for pavement, stores, some place she recognized. Something besides the ugliness of the place and the stink of herself.

In the last days, Sarah had often found her mother in the blue chair by the bay window next to the garden, where she'd come to sit in the middle of the night. "It is so dark," she'd say. "I wanted to be by the window when morning came." Her mother had held her father's hands and said, "I'm going home now. I'm ready to go home." Her father, broken, had said, "I love you." Sarah had held her mother's hand, crying, "Mommy, don't go!" The terrain was shadowy and unfamiliar. The alleys led to more alleys and Sarah hoped for a street with sidewalks and rickshaws and vegetable sellers. The people lurking in these tin shacks were not the ones who spoke English. She was turning in circles and choking in her own smell and couldn't speak Gujarati well enough to ask for help. The running and her fear raised hotness in her head and in her chest. When what you counted on vanished, anything could happen. Her fear was crumbling her from the inside out; she wanted to curl up on a mattress with the little children and let someone take care of her. Wake when it was over. When she was out of the muddle of darkness, the slum where life and death mingled so effortlessly.

Sarah ran, looking for the opening.

Gandhi, bent, bespectacled, bronzed stood before her on a pedestal in the middle of a square. His neck was adorned with marigold garlands and his bald head shone. Sarah knew this place. Up ahead a woman, whose rich brown mid-drift escaped above her sari skirt, was throwing open the shutters of a small whitewashed shop. She wore silk of purples and greens. Thick forearms jingled with shiny silver bangles. She was Lisa's tailor, the one who had laughed.

"Namaste," Sarah called out, her own voice a shock, her body melting with relief.

"Namaste!" The woman pressed her palms together in greeting and looked hard at Sarah. "Aha! The girl from the scooter, is it?" Her English was lilting.

"I fell when I was running and I smell horrible, I'm afraid. I don't know which way the Vidyapith is."

"Please do come in for a cup of tea." The woman's shiny black hair was twisted in a tight bun above her fine featured face. "My husband and I run a tailor, you know." She pointed with pride to a small sign in Gujarati and English.

"I'll be late." Sarah looked at her watch. "I have a meeting."

"We don't hurry in India. Drink some tea and I'll dab your pants."

Sarah looked at the street behind her, Gandhi's hopeful face and firm stride, a tired dog, a trash collector with a wagon of scraps, a maze of streets leading into the square. She stood for a second. The woman had gone in the shop.

Inside, the woman held out a glass of hot chai. A small altar with incense burning hung on a wall and there was a statue of a lotus-positioned god on a shelf. A bright poster of Princess Di hung on another wall. Against the far wall bolts of colorful material were neatly stacked. In the center of the room, a worktable held a shiny black and silver Singer sewing machine.

"You can't wear those pants."

"They smell. I know." Sarah sipped the sweet hot tea.

"No, my dear, you just can't wear them. Not becoming. Not flattering. They are what peasant men wear." She lifted Sarah's shirt and reached in to pinch. "And, they make you look even skinnier than you are. No. No. This will not do." She stood back and circled Sarah.

"How long are you here?" the woman finally asked.

"Here? Six more weeks. Until Christmas."

"No. *Here*." She held her smooth palms up, "This shop."

Sarah put down her tea glass. "I have a meeting at ten with some sweepers. Very good tea." She held out the glass to the woman but it was not taken.

"Sweepers. Now that is interesting."

"Thank you again but I need to go."

"What do you find interesting about the sweepers?" The woman was pulling out a tape measure, scissors, unfolding a metal chair.

"They've formed a cooperative. They're demanding better conditions and healthcare."

"Things are different from America, is it?" The woman took the glass from Sarah now and put it on the table.

"Not as much as you'd think. But that's not it really." Sarah felt flushed from the tea, the heat from the stove.

"What then?" The woman was raising Sarah's arms into a T and measuring around her bust and her waist.

"I'm not sure." Sarah tried to put her arms down but the woman skillfully measured her shoulders.

"I wonder," the woman said, "if it's their rotten luck. They take their rotten luck and make something better."

Sarah looked at her, this woman whose name she didn't know.

"Now, raise up your arms again. We have time."

"No. I haven't time," Sarah said. But her arms were lifted.

"I'm making a beautiful sari for you. My gift to the American girl."

"I've got to get back." Sarah tried again to leave, but the woman held her arm with firm fingers.

"It is bad luck to refuse a gift." She took a piece of material and held it out. "A sari is just a very long piece of beautiful material. Tucked and pleated just so. I will quickly sew you a blouse and I have a sari slip you can have. This last piece just comes up over your shoulder."

The woman efficiently began cutting, her back to Sarah. Sometimes Sarah wanted to slap someone, Roger, her mother, this woman. She couldn't believe that this woman had so skillfully trapped her. But exhaustion overcame her. Sarah felt pinned to the floor but suddenly safe.

"My name is Surya and you are?"

"Sarah," she whispered.

"Sarah, come look at the lovely silks." Surya turned. "Oh, oh, I see. Sadness is there." She made a clucking sound with her tongue and pulled a white handkerchief from a fold in her sari and pressed into Sarah's hand. "I see, dear. Sometimes, I think, a sari can make us feel beautiful, graceful." She pulled down a rich bolt of cloth.

The room was snug and quiet. The sari slip was over the back of the chair. Sarah untied the drawstring on her pants, rolled them into a ball and put on the slip.

Surya pressed Sarah gently into the chair. She refilled the glass with steaming chai and placed it between Sarah's palms.

"You look at the cloth, OK? I'll sew your blouse while you choose your sari."

The warmth of the glass tingled Sarah's hands.

"I went to the river this morning; they were going to wash and burn a body."

"Where Lord Shiva ferries them to the far shore." Surya paused and pointed to the god on her shelf. "Shiva. We say that death is certain for all who are born, and birth is certain for the dead."

"I thought that Shiva was the destroyer."

"But it is never-ending. From destruction comes creation."

"I guess." Sarah listened.

"In the Bhagavad Gita Krishna says the cycle is inevitable, so there is no cause for grief. Death is a passage, we believe. It doesn't mean there isn't sadness. But it isn't the end."

She felt her shoulder blades melt downward. Surya bent over the sewing machine, guiding the piece of cloth surely under the darting needle. The humming noise made Sarah sleepy. Her mother had a Singer. It was probably in a case in the closet still. They used to sew clothes for Sarah's dolls. Little smocked party dresses. A pink and white striped bathrobe for Molly, the favorite doll, to match Sarah's. A snowsuit so Molly could play outside.

Sarah closed her eyes. She was upstairs in her parents' bedroom where the sewing table faced the leafy maples and oaks in the backyard. On rainy Sundays when she was younger her mother would snuggle in bed with her while her father made omelets downstairs. If they didn't feel like going to church her mother would say, let's just go for a walk later. Her mother said God was in the small rocks and shells they used to hunt for at Race Point in the summer, in the tapping of the woodpecker in the mountain ash, in the thunderheads that swept in during the spring. And, her mother would say, what about a Lady Slipper?

Her mother had been a dabbler, a noticer of small things. She'd built strange sculptures out of scrap metal and planted them in the front yard. She tutored children, knit stocking caps, learned how to paint sunsets from a PBS show, took modern dance at the church and told Sarah, "Look at me; I'm a mountain, now a river, now a cloud." She'd gone on roller coasters when dared. What had once made her magical made her an object of disdain when Sarah became a teen.

She'd been flighty, fanciful and lacked focus, seriousness, a sense of the heaviness of the world. And look what had happened.

Sarah could feel the warmth of someone standing near. Her mother had sweet and salty breath that puffed over her like steam from a kettle. She wanted a boiled egg sitting like a head in the body of a dancing woman. She wanted to eat it slowly, with a spoon, flooded by the light coming in the square panes of the kitchen window. She wanted to dance in a golden sari in the courtyard of the Vidyapith. She wanted someone to unwrap her. She wanted the hurt to start so the numbness would end. She wanted to believe her mother again and feel her light. A lady slipper, her mother, would say, God in a flower.

Warm salty trails curved over her lips. She felt like a glacier, calving, breaking apart and falling into the ocean. The folding metal chair on the cement floor on the red earth a million miles from anywhere was where she was. Look at me; I'm a mountain, now a river, now a cloud.

Green Line

The Green Line train stopped in the tunnel somewhere between Copley and Arlington. A tiny spider of tension bit just under Adam's breastbone and pulsed outward. *Hyperarousal*, Dr. Davies called it. Adam wished Humphrey was next to him. Sometimes he just lay with Humphrey on his dog bed and breathed with him until the rise and fall of their bodies synced. "Battle mind kept you alive, Adam. But you can release it now." Yeah.

Adam turned and caught the eyes of the girl he'd given his seat to at Chestnut Hill. His knees were flush against her baby's stroller. The baby had looked hot and ready to wail, the mother stressed out, wrangling the stroller through the train. He'd waited a beat to see if someone else would offer her a seat first.

The girl's skin was a light brown color—Italian, Mexican, Iraqi, who knew—and her black hair was twisted up and stuck through with little chop-sticks. She didn't even look twenty. Her white tank top had a small mustard stain on it. She was pretty. Whenever the girl reached up to touch her hair or to give her baby the stump of his bagel, Adam squinted to read the tattoo on her inner arm. The tattoo was small and in cursive. The last three words were *in my grave*, but he couldn't see what came before. The girl chewed on her pinky nail and looked away.

What she saw: her own reflection in the window, everyone else around her all colors and shapes and sizes, like they were the pulsing insides of the metal beast. And what was *he* freaking staring at?

The train vibrated spastically as if it might lurch forward. Adam held on tighter and pulled his eyes away from the girl's eyes and looked at his watch. Please, don't fucking die on me, train. Or explode. In the stroller, the baby chugged up to a restless cry. Adam felt the same restlessness building in him. How could time crawl and speed at the same time? If he didn't get to Esme's by 8:15, he probably wouldn't get to see Lily. Adam touched the envelope with the $451—six $50's, five $20's, five $10's and a silver dollar he had traded quarters for at the bank. He hoped Esme would say, "Your Daddy wanted you to have this."

The baby's unsettled energy was contagious. The other passengers thumbed newspapers, fiddled with iPods, or looked outside to the dark tunnel where the train shuddered in place. The girl gave her baby a finger to grab, and he dropped the soggy bagel somewhere in the folds of his blanket. Adam felt dizzy and held on to the metal bar tighter, feeling as if they were moving though he knew they weren't. How can you know one thing and feel another? He got Goddamn annoyed at himself when this happened.

The conductor came on overhead and said something about removing something on the tracks—'did he say body?' 'debris' 'what did he say?' 'I'm going to be so fucking late'—and that they'd be moving momentarily. Moving and Removing. Removing and Moving. What was the difference? Removing—moving something that is not supposed to be there or that you don't want. IEDs when you could find them, bodies when you could not. A splinter from Esme's palm with his tongue and teeth, in those days when she let him touch her anytime any place. Lily, facing backwards in her car seat, with her starfish hand on the window. *It's way past your last chance, Adam.* Adam felt the dark hole under his sternum, the place where he held all the tears and terror. He wouldn't make the mistake of falling into that dark pit again. A-B-C-D-E-F-Geeee, H-I-J-K, LMNOP. Singing to himself. Careful not to move his lips or bob his head. It helped, sometimes.

The train began to stutter forward and pick up speed. The girl rested her head against the window with her eyes closed. The baby tipped his face to peer up at him, a goofy look in his big brown eyes. Peek-a-boo. The baby froze, like it couldn't decide whether to scream or laugh and then stiffened all his limbs and shrieked.

The girl startled upright and scanned her eyes like mine sweepers over the car.

What she saw: a white haired woman in a pink muumuu closing her *People* magazine and sliding it into the plastic shopping bag at her feet; a boy with his pants low on his hips cracking his knuckles and swaying side to side to rhythms only he could hear; the tall brown-haired man who'd given her his seat, looking nervous. Her intuition about people was usually sharp (the one major exception being James' father, but she got James so maybe it was meant to be). Something in the way that guy arranged his face into blankness made her pick up her baby just to feel his plump warm body collapse into hers.

Adam slipped his hand into his pocket again to feel the thick envelope of cash. *You have no more obligations.* Esme had made that clear. He felt something had crawled inside his body and claimed it. A parasite. He even looked it up, once. *An organism that grows, feeds, and is sheltered on or in a different organism while contributing nothing to the survival of its host.*

He watched the baby gnawing on its mother's shoulder. What would it feel like to mouth that smooth brown knob of skin? Or lower down. Her nipples poked through her t-shirt. He waited for a twitch of hot wanting, practically said a prayer over it. Nada.

The train shrieked into Arlington station. Sparks on the rails. Fireworks between his temples. He put his fingers there. Two more stops until changing to the Red Line. He squinted at the map overhead. The doors opened and people began to push out. The girl collapsed the stroller with one arm while holding the baby on her hip and moved toward the doors. Sadness that she was leaving, that everyone leaves, invaded his chest. The damp bagel and a set of crayon-colored plastic keys fell to the floor. Adam scooped them up in his free hand and called, "You dropped something, Miss!" She was on the platform now. He slid through the doors just when they started to shut. "Here. You dropped these." He heard the doors whoosh close and felt the heat from the train and the summer day sucking at him as the train drew away. Her face turned toward him, plucked brows making a "V", face flushed and closed. For a beat, a pause, the tick of the second hand on his watch closer to 8:15, he thought she might turn away. She was calculating risk; he got that.

"Oh. Hold on a sec." She rattled the stroller open and buckled the baby in. "Yuck. Sorry you had to touch that." She removed the bagel from his palm and the plastic key ring from his finger. The tips of her fingers heated his skin.

"Well." She dangled the keys for her baby. "Thanks then."

Esme had said more than once, "You intimidate people when you're so quiet. At least babble. Babbling is better than nothing." She'd rap him on the skull sometimes or run her hand over his crew cut, "What the fuck goes on in there?" Dr. Davies said, "When a thought or a feeling arises, try to see it existing in lots of space. You don't have to follow every thought."

Thought: *Lily. I might miss her.*

Thought: *What does your tattoo say?*

Thought: *There was an Iraqi girl with a sweet crooked smile like yours. And soft hands.*

Thought: *I need to leave.*

The girl began to back up a little, tugging on her stroller. "Ok then. Thanks again."

What she thought: He's a little weird. Or slow maybe. Yeah.

She began to move toward the turnstiles.

"It was no problem. I've got a daughter." He gestured toward the tracks. "I'm going to see her now." His love for Lily was this huge strange thing that almost strangled him when he said her name out loud.

"That was nice of you to get off the train then. He loves those keys." The baby was wetly mouthing them.

"Looks like he couldn't be happier." Adam saw that when he said this, it was true. In the hot subway station with newspapers fluttering by the trash can, the slight smell of French fries in the air and the darkness pulling both ways, the baby, really, was happy.

"Where can I get me some of that, huh?" She fluttered her arm goodbye and he saw the words *Your memory will not die in my grave.*

The road ahead ripped and steamed skyward, clipping the back of the Humvee, a mayhem of metal and billows of black smoke. *Will anyone remember? What's happening, Adam?* He'd lifted Eddie's head and slid his own thigh under to pillow it. Something soft underneath, not just the sand, wet with Eddie's blood and whatever other shit was coming out of his head. Adam was in the Humvee behind Eddie's, obscured now and then by clouds of sand and dust when the wind picked up, but rumbling along. Then—

The Sergeant yelled, "Stay with him till the medics get here." He would have gone anyway, through the smoking voids where a second ago was road. He held Eddie's hand while everything leaked out. He went with Eddie for a while, wherever Eddie went on his mind's last odyssey. *What's happening to me, what's happening here?* Ann Marie, Jack, his father's gold wrist watch, an Eagle Scout badge for Citizenship in the World, some girl he ditched, promises unfilled, sins of omission, black holes of pain—Oh Jesus!

The vibration of the ground under his feet staggered him back to a bench. It was only the next Green Line train. He waited for the doors to open and the people to disembark.

He took the stairs at the Porter Street station two at a time. Most people were going the other way, sucked in toward the city with laptops and handbags slung around their bodies like he used to wear his M40. By the time he got to the top, he was panting, the muggy mid-June air close in and dampening his t-shirt to his body. That's the thing he needed to ask the doctor. Could a hammering heart break free, break out of the ribs—delicate, he's seen some—a torrent of blood? And would it be a death or a liberation? He should have stayed at home. Should have stayed underground at least. Except for walking Humphrey, he didn't do much to stay in shape. Not like some of the guys he saw strutting around the West Roxbury VA, still jacked, the blue veins in their forearms swollen, their *death before dishonor* tattoos twitching when they lifted their coffee cups. Before his first tour, he'd had Esme's name tattooed on the inside of his right wrist. When he put his hand to his heart, she was close up against it. When Lily was born, he had her name inked inside the left. When he prayed—*dear God get me the fuck out of here*—they were all three together like that. Dear God. *Dear God.* Nada.

Adam stopped at the street corner and pulled his pack of Marlboro reds from his t-shirt pocket. His hands were still trembling and the match jumped around a bit before he got the cigarette lit. Being in the army turned him into a smoker. Most of them came home smokers if they weren't when they got there. No time to sleep? Smoke. Bored? Smoke. Saw your life pass before your eyes? Smoke. Sometimes he'd close his eyes and picture freeing the smoke from his mouth in great loopy rings for Esme to put her fingers through.

He drew in deeply, following the sharp burn of smoke down to where it dissipated inside him, unleashing its microscopic cancers and calming powers, both offering something. Just a couple more blocks down Elm Street and then a right on something-er-other. Not Cherry but the one after. Then, left to where they lived. Third little house on the right. He could see it in his mind's eye. The shaking in his hands settled as he moved. He had a sweet rush—the nicotine and a feeling of having escaped danger, of the worst not having come to pass, not this time, at least. There were moments when he'd return to base after particularly fucked up missions and feel completely weightless, like the 73 pounds of clothing and body armor and gear was air.

At the stoplight at the corner of Elm and Cedar, a school bus—Somerville Public Schools—waited at the red light. Lily's bus didn't come down Cedar, did it? But his watch read 8:03 and he picked up the pace. Pick up the pace. Pick up the pace. Pick up the pieces. Average White Band. Now he had that song in his head. Earwigs, that's what they called songs that got stuck like that. He'd played tenor sax to *Pick up the Pieces* in 8th grade—the harmony, Mr. Tillotson said. The hard part because when he'd practiced it over and over at home it didn't sound like the song. Maybe Lily would play an instrument someday. Piano. Or flute. He always liked watching the girls—their fingers fluttering like moths—over the little silver keys.

One black high top sneaker lay on its side in the gutter, the gum colored sole turned skyward. How do you lose just one shoe? Or, maybe it belonged to someone who'd already lost a foot or a leg. Maybe this person had stuffed all the shoes he didn't need into a garbage bag and this one slipped out. He shook his head as if this would jar loose the stories that accumulated in it; distractions. No, worse than that. Trash. Crap that just clogged up his brain.

A bicycle messenger almost clipped Adam as the bike jetted by on the sidewalk, startling him. He felt like lobbing the lost shoe at the rider who moved so easily, as if there were no obstacles. His mother once said when he was about 11 years old, "My name is not Look-Ma-No-Hands!" He field stripped the cigarette and flicked the filter into the next trash can he saw. He broke into a little jog, the pressure of the envelope against his thigh now irritating. He couldn't wait to hand it to Esme, couldn't wait to be done with wondering how Esme would look at him. Done with wondering if Brian would be there, blocking the door with his stocky body.

He turned onto their street, a street of duplexes, the caged lawns mostly trimmed and neat with occasional pots of flowers on the steps or maybe the Virgin Mary settled in the yard. The last time he'd come, a couple of the houses had still had Easter decorations up—eggs hanging from trees, or little wooden bunnies staked to the ground. That time he'd brought some seedlings—cosmos, sunflowers, sal-via—from the greenhouse at the VA where he "worked" one afternoon a week with some other jumpy vets. One guy freaked out whenever they had a plant sale. Separation anxiety or something. Adam liked the greenhouses, mostly for the smell of the warm damp air that fired up memories of summers when he actually didn't want the days to end.

He stood at the bottom of the four cement steps that led up to the stoop, the door. A white window box below the living room bay window displayed a jumble of purple and pink petunias. Probably they'd planted the flowers he'd left in pots in the backyard. He put his hand on the railing. Waiting.

What she saw: Him. Him? Standing at the bottom of the steps. Blue t-shirt tucked into his jeans; neat. Thinner and ropier than ever, looking like some lost dog. Contrary to what he thought, she never gave up. Just gave out. In the kitchen, Lily's spoon clicked against her cereal bowl. Esme could hear the sound of the TV news drifting from upstairs. She had really fucking loved him until she couldn't anymore.

She opened the door.

"What do you want?"

The last time she didn't even open the door, she just hollered through it. He was advancing.

"I just want to see Lily." Disarm her. Charm her. Her hair was a little longer, her cheeks a little chubbier. "Is she here?"

She shook her head No. He scanned the windows. Living room bay window—glare. Upstairs window left—frosted; bathroom? Upstairs window right—open three inches and pink curtains inflating and deflating gently in the breeze like lungs.

"She left already?" He squinted his eyes. Was the enemy being truthful? She turned away from him and put her hand with its tiny chip of diamond on her belly.

"Adam. You're not supposed to be here." Unofficial but agreed upon. Until the day when he really got his shit together. "You need to leave."

What she remembered: His white body like a canvas, the sun through the window slats painting shimmering bands of light and shadow on him. The scar in the middle of his chest from some childhood mishap. Drops of water from the shower sparkling on him. Desire pinning them against the wall like they were riding the Gravitron at the fair. She sat down on the stoop and put her face in her hands.

It was so sad to see her so sad, and he bit his lip hard, a trick or a tic he'd developed to keep himself from the edge. He came up one step.

"Stop." She put out her hand.

"Did Lily like to play peek-a-boo when she was a baby?" How could a father not know this? He was embarrassed by the catch in his voice.

Her forehead had a little sheen of sweat.

"Yes." She pulled herself up by the railing.

Jesus she was pregnant. That's what.

"Where are the flowers I left last time?"

"What?" She shook her head. "Last time? What're you talking about?"

"Six packs of cosmos, salvia, sunflowers." He gestured toward the step. "I left them right here."

"You've been coming here?" She reached back and put her hand on the screen door. "You're not supposed to come here. We agreed. Until...."

Which he hadn't. They both knew. Gotten his shit together.

He widened his sight; he could do that from laser sharp beams to wide spotlights. He took in everything. The roof. The windows. The puffing pink curtains. Her face. His hands.

"You need to go now, Adam." Very softly she said it.

His heart was beating so loud; could she hear it? There was a trick to stilling it and your breath. When he learned she'd remarried, he didn't spill a drop from the glass in his hands.

"I want to see Lily."

What she felt: Her heart was beating so hard she felt crazy. There was a time when she could curl around him at night and everything would calm inside her. She'd plod down into sleep following the steady thump of his heart. Then, over time, only the shell of his body was what was familiar anymore.

She would not resort to calling Brian; Adam knew this the way soldiers are taught to know things, by instinct. But she was retreating from him again, coming just enough far forward each time so the tight place where he held hope unzipped just a little bit more. She'd slipped inside so quickly and now the screen was between them, now the solid oak door. In a driveway behind him, an engine revved. A car alarm sing-songed. Above him, the pink curtains hung still now, as if a door had been shut in an upstairs bedroom. Adam stood for a second where she'd left him. His hand trembled as he pulled the envelope from his pocket. Breathing slowly, moving as if underwater.

What she saw: The man from the picture with green eyes just like hers. He came home from far away to meet her when she was a baby. Then he left for far away again, and when he came home for real, he was all broken, too broken. That was all she knew. But it was him; she knew it the first time she saw him in their yard. She held the curtains so she could peek. He put something on the top step and then began his leaving, like he did every time, stepping almost exactly where he had on the way up.

Unleashed

Her dog Ike pulls on the leash attached to Alison's wrist as Thomas, her son, holds on to the back of her coat and her purse slides to the crook of her arm. Alison feels stretched and off balance. Before entering the nursing home, she needs to right herself.

"Hold my hand," she says, unclenching Thomas' small fist from the back of her winter coat. She wets a finger and rubs a blob of peanut butter from his cheek.

"Smile. Okay?" They count on us to help them forget, she thinks. Thomas is four. He goes where she goes. His cool little hand in hers keeps her grounded.

"Heel. Heel." Alison pulls on Ike's leash as she opens the door.

Rule #1 of the Pet Visiting Program: Control and Protect Your Pet. Alison fears Ike could hurt himself or others in his great bounding happiness; knock down an elderly person on a walker or grow tangled in the wires and tubes that encircle some of the more infirmed residents.

Linda, the nursing home activities director, calls from down the long beige hallway, "The guests are so excited you're here! They're all waiting for your visit!" The word *guests* catches Alison off-guard, as if the old folks are just here for a little getaway—as if they have a choice. Linda's enthusiasm is overwhelming and genuine. Her optimism shames Alison. This was not a good day to come, perhaps. *You have the winter blues*, her husband said, kissing her temple that morning. But it's almost the end of March.

At the sound of a low familiar whistle, Ike pricks up his ears and lunges. Alison's wrist is exposed and she can see her Timex, the one with timers and alarms and splits for working out, something she hasn't done in months. A half an hour max, she tells herself. Then they need to pick up Luke and Isabel from elementary school and get them to piano lessons and gymnastics.Russell is waiting for them in his wheel chair at the end of the hallway near the nurses' station. He is always the first to greet them, toeing his wheel chair over the shiny linoleum toward them. When he puts four fingers in his mouth to whistle again, Alison runs her tongue over her own teeth, glad for them. Russell slumps in his wheel chair as if the bones of his spine have been ground to sand. His face reminds her of those Richard Nixon Halloween masks. But, Alison watches as Russell, straining toward Ike as eagerly as Ike strains toward him, lights up, lifts up even for a moment. She experiences a feeling of lightness in herself. Yes.

"Good boy. Good boy." Russell's thick knuckled hands rub behind Ike's ears. Ike's tail slashes back and forth against Thomas's ankles, and he giggles. Russell reaches into his sweatshirt pocket and pulls out chunks of donuts which Ike snarfs up.

Rule #2 of the Pet Visiting Program: Get Down on Their Level. Alison stoops down by Russell's knee and puts her arm around Ike's neck to keep him from leaping into Russell's lap, strewn with donut crumbs. Thomas throws his body across Alison's back. She's hot. The brightness and heat pulsing out of the lights and the radiator vents make her feel like the chicks the kids hatched in a little incubator last spring, ready to shed the shell, ready to fly the coop.

"Oh I missed this dog! You haven't brought him in a long time!" Russell's voice sounds like it is coming from a meat grinder.

"He missed you, too. Look at him." We come as often as we can, Alison thinks, feeling a little prick of guilt.

Russell reaches out a palm to offer Thomas a bite of donut, too. Before Alison can protest, Thomas stretches his neck and flickers out his tongue.

"Thomas!" Alison stands up. Thomas looks up at her with those big green impish eyes and swallows.

"Do you know I've got two German short-hairs?" Russell asks, as he does every time. "I love those dogs." For a second, he rests his empty hands in his lap. A quiver of drool leaves his lip. "Oh I miss 'em." He shakes his head.

"But you can't remember their names!" Thomas announces. It's true; they go through this each time.

"It's okay, Russell," Alison says, "I can't remember a lot of things either."

Did I take the chicken out to defrost?

She reaches out a hand to pat Russell's shoulder. It shocks her how it feels like there is nothing between the skin and the bone, as if essential parts of him have just disappeared.

An orderly blasts by with a bucket of sudsy water and a splash hits the top of Alison's clogs.

Did I leave the house unlocked for the cleaning lady?

She remembers leaving the check. But, in the bustle of combing the dog and changing her clothes and finding Thomas's favorite hat.... There is soap scum on the door of the shower in the master bath, and she wants the window sills vacuumed before she puts in the screens. Last night after the kids were asleep, she headed into the kids bathroom with rubber gloves and a bottle of 409. Her husband called from their bedroom, "What are you doing now? Come and tell me about your day, honey." She squirted some cleaner in the sink and looked into the mirror. "How was my day?" She had no answer.

"Okay, Thomas. Shall we say goodbye to Russell?"

The old man is looking up toward the ceiling, or maybe into his own brain, as if he could retrieve the names of his dogs there. Sadness drags him further down into his wheelchair. He knows enough to know he has forgotten something he swore he'd never forget.

How old was Thomas when he took his first step?

A food cart pushed by a headphone-wearing teen in pink scrubs skitters by and down the shiny hall. Alison pulls her little entourage to the side, just in time. Ike's nose twitches after the cart and he starts to pull. Over her shoulder Alison calls, "We'll see you next time Russell. Okay?" He is brushing crumbs off his lap and looks up and salutes them.

Alison and the dog and Thomas pause at the door of the next room. An Asian woman with a fuzz of white hair and a tiny O of a mouth sits in a rocking chair by the window with a pile of Fig Newtons in her lap. She shakes her head and flaps her hands to send them away. Her roommate is a wisp of a woman with a face the color of butter who has been asleep at every visit. Ahead of the game, Alison thinks, to maybe sleep through your last days, if this is what they are.

"Would you like a little visit with our dog today, Mrs."—Alison squints at the name plate by the door—"Tang?"

"No. No. No." The old woman shakes her head again. Her glasses slide off her nose and are caught by the chain around her neck. She covers the Fig Newtons with her hands. Despite the fact that the nurse told them that Mrs. Tang can't even remember her name most days,

Mrs. Tang seems to recall that Ike gulped a cookie off her lap during their last, aborted visit.

Rule #3: Respect their Wishes. Some people may be allergic to or afraid of your pet.

On the wall outside Mrs. Tang's room, someone has created a collage. In the middle, there is a photo of Mrs. Tang. Her short black hair is stylishly cut. She's wearing a simple white blouse with pearls and red pants. Standing shoulder to shoulder with her is a hand-some Chinese man in a business suit. They are both resting their hands on the shoulders of three little girls, all of whom are wearing blue pleated skirts and sharp white blouses. The girls are beaming, as if the photographer has promised them a puppy when the photo shoot is over. Mrs. Tang looks like she's suppressing a smile and her eyes are wide, as if she's taking it all in, as if she doesn't want to blink and miss a thing.

"What, Momma?" Thomas asks.

"See the pictures of Mrs. Tang before she lived here?" She points to the radiant and young version of Mrs. Tang. Surrounding this center picture are other photos: Mrs. Tang holding a ping pong paddle in one hand and a trophy in the other. Mrs. Tang alone on the top of a mountain, the wind blowing her short hair, the sun shining in her eyes. Mrs. Tang giving a kiss to a young woman in a cap and gown. A gray-haired and beaming Mr. and Mrs. Tang each holding an infant—twin grandbabies?—in each arm. A white haired Mrs. Tang in a pink sweater cutting dahlias in an endless radiant garden.

Like Thomas, Alison turns her gaze from the photo collage on the wall and into the room where Mrs. Tang pitches back and forth in her chair by the window.

"They's the same person?" Thomas gasps.

"She." Alison corrects absently as she looks for some snap and sparkle in the Mrs. Tang by the window. "She is the same person."

Alison tries to picture Thomas, his flashing green eyes, the tender spray of freckles, his whole four-year-old being nothing but snap and sparkle, 80 years hence. It's like someone put a feather in one palm and a stone in the other and said, *These are the same.*

She takes Thomas' hand and clucks at Ike to keep moving. She cannot bear at this moment to picture old man Thomas and all the loss and heartbreak and loneliness he will endure, without her there holding his hand. Could the Mrs. Tang with the triumphant smile and the uplifted trophy be the same agitated Mrs. Tang with her lapful of cookies?

Maybe Thomas is right. She is they. We are many.

They pass by a ceiling vent blowing hot dry air.

"Hold on a sec." Alison puts the leash in Thomas' hand, unbuttons her wool coat and flaps it open and closed like a fan. "Hot," she says and reclaims the leash. Thomas looks at her, unzips his little red jacket and slips it off on to the floor.

"Whoa Doodlebug! Can you pick up that jacket? Here, hand it to me." He's been such a good boy. She'll get him a treat afterwards. M&Ms; he loves those.

Thomas swoops up his jacket and tosses it onto her outstretched arm.

Ike, nose down, strains toward the next room. Flora's back is to them, her fine auburn hair neatly coiffed. The bed nearest the door is empty. The nightstand holds only a box of tissues. Alison can't conjure up who used to be here.

Alison calls gently from the door, "Good morning Flora. It's your dog visitor." The three of them navigate widely and carefully into the room.

Flora turns her head from where she stares into the parking lot. Today she is wearing a thick cable knit purple cardigan with silver buttons and camel colored pants. She always looks so put together. Someone visits weekly, it appears, to take her to get her hair and nails done. The first time they visited, Alison for the life of her couldn't figure out why a woman, who looked like she could still work behind the counter at a Talbots, or command a board room, was in a place like this.

"Well hello! Hello young man!" Flora extends her wrinkled hand like a queen would, as if Thomas should kiss the large diamond and ruby ring sparkling on her middle finger. The boy eyes Flora but squeezes the bones in his mother's hand. Ike sniffs at Flora's knees.

"Good morning, Flora. You look lovely today." Alison gently transfers Thomas' hand to Flora's for a little shake.

Flora smiles as Thomas' plump little paw squeezes her fingers. Then she blurts, "Who are you anyway, by the way, today, zebras are gray?"

That's what happened the first time they visited. As though she's been slapped silly, Flora begins to talk nonsense and then plunges into some murky place as if the gray matter of her brain is the contents of a whirring blender.

"No don't tell me!" Flora puts a finger coyly on her cheek. "I'm going to guess who you are!" Her eyes scamper from Alison to Thomas and back and forth again.

"When we were down on the farm picking blueberries, you—" she points a rosy nail at Thomas—"took my bucket and I told Mama on you." Her face gets pouty.

Alison watches Thomas carefully. It is a lot to ask, these visits. He stares, his arms limp by his sides, and yawns vastly.

"I'm hungry."

"There are LifeSavers in the bottom of my purse." She hands her purse to Thomas, and he wanders to sit on the edge of the bed with it. Her watch says time is almost up.

"And you.... are my niece. Yes." Flora nods. She's gotten hold of something she likes.

"No. No Flora," Alison shakes her head. "I'm Alison. With the dog. The pet visitors." She squats down, takes Flora's hand, gives it a little shake, as if to wake Flora up out of her dream. She feels the surprising lightness of bone and softness of skin. She pinches Flora's palm.

"Ouch! O dear that hurts." Flora looks confused, but then she gives her head a quick snap. "I always loved that about you! Impish. Your mother might give you a good spanking though."

Thomas has moved to the window, the pack of Lifesavers clutched in his palm. He is blowing steam on the glass. Ike sits by Flora's chair.

The visits with Flora always take this turn and Alison is freshly startled—and to tell the truth—angered by it each time. *Why am I angry? It's not her fault.*

She pulls a chair from the corner and sits down on the edge, exhausted. She is tired of explaining the unexplainable to children who need facts and truth. She is tired of separating darks from lights and sorting by item, in pairs, by child. She is tired of preparing food balanced by color and texture and taste. She is tired of creating order in cupboards and closets and days. She's tired of always looking at her watch and wondering where else she should be.

Bright flashing lights make them all turn toward the window. An ambulance slowly pulls up to the entrance.

"Coming for someone again." Flora's face deflates and her eyes look like Russell's when he can't remember the names of his dogs. Then she throws that off as quickly as it came on. "I'm just here while they fix my car. I'm going home any time. I am a lucky one."

Rule #4 Don't Argue with People's Version of Reality.

Maybe that's not a rule, but it should be.

"Down boy." Ike obeys and lays his big golden body on the floor. Alison puts her elbows on her knees, leaning in toward Flora.

"When I was little....Aunt Flora...." why not, she thinks? "What was I like?"

"Hoo yoo! I've got stories to tell." When she smiles her teeth are like little pearls, and her face shines on Alison.

"Tell me something now." Alison feels like she might start crying. Who is she to pity Flora? When it comes down to it, Flora finds ways to spring her own trap, to create a reality that frees her for a moment.

Thomas sits on the bed and unspools the foil wrapper around the Lifesavers.

"I can tell you this; we are a lot alike, you and I," Flora says. "Everyone always said so."

"How so Flora?" Alison looks intently at Flora, at the crooked skim of lipstick on her upper lip, at the flashing lights behind her head, signaling desperation and saving all at once.

"You know what?" Flora looks at Thomas and points her finger, "You were just like that!"

Thomas is lying on the bed, staring up at the ceiling and gnashing a mouthful of wintergreen Lifesavers, with gusto.

Alison feels the heaviness of her good winter coat pressing down on her shoulders. She shrugs it off and lets it slide down the back of the chair. She does remember being like Thomas. She remembers putting four rolls of Wintergreen Lifesavers in her pocket and quietly climbing up the stairs and over the green shag carpeting to the kids' bathroom when she was not much older than he. She'd heard they sparkled fluorescently if you chewed them with your mouth open in the dark. In the bathroom, she turned out the light and pulled the curtains her mother made against the late summer light. How wonderful it would be to see lights and sparkles coming out of her. She'd stood in front of the mirror in the pitch dark and did it over and over until her mother called her for dinner.

What Is the Color Blue?

Claire put her hands on the old barn door and opened it just a bit. The air inside smelled of nesting mice and the lingering leather scent of a barn once full of horses. Gray liquid light snuck in through the gaps and the missing panes of glass, illuminating an old stool, tufts of hay, and scatterings of grains that cracked under Claire's feet. Holly ran for the stool and stood on it.

"Look, Mom, I'm almost as tall as you," Holly said.

Claire opened her arms, and Holly jumped into them.

The barn and old house were just down the road from where they lived, and they had been for sale for months. Yesterday a SOLD! sign appeared. When Biscuit, their dog, shot off after a flock of turkeys in the field behind the barn, Claire thought it might be their last chance to snoop about the place.

"It's nice to think that someone bought this house, isn't it?" Claire said, as they walked back outside. Holly ran and puddle-jumped in her black rubber boots. The lifting rain gave way to sun. Claire tied her blue rain coat around her waist, called for Biscuit, and they started for home.

At the edge of the driveway, a black Jeep with the top down and New York plates idled by the mailbox. In the driver's seat, a woman with a sweep of blond hair fiddled with something in her lap.

"Oh hey!" The woman looked up as they approached the top of the driveway. She turned off the Jeep and stepped out, a camera with a long lens in her hand. "I'm Isabel," she said, side stepping a puddle in her high-heeled boots.

"Are you the new owner? I'm Claire and this is my daughter Holly." Claire felt disheveled in her gardening jeans and sweatshirt. Isabel wore a white blouse and an elegant black jacket. The sun caught the gold hoops in her ears. Claire had forgotten to put in earrings this morning.

"My husband and I just bought this place. Glorious isn't it?" Isabel was stunning, with her sharp cheekbones and brown eyes flecked with gold. "Are you a neighbor?"

Claire smoothed the curls in her hair. "You just passed our house. One field that-away."

"Wonderful." Isabel squatted eye-to-eye with Holly. "How old are you? My daughter Darcy will be coming up later today with her dad and the horses."

"Seven." Holly smiled, looking Isabel in the eye. Claire loved her daughter's confidence; admired it.

"Darcy's eight! Oh, this is going to be everything I hoped for!" Isabel stood up and held out her camera, gold bangles shimmering on her wrists. "Do you mind if I take your picture? Maybe just scooch nearer the stone wall and then I can get some of the house and barn behind you. And those mountains, too."

They did as they were told. Even Biscuit sat for a moment.

"I'm so excited to be getting out of New York and moving to Vermont," Isabel said from behind her camera.

"It's different than the city, of course," Claire said, her arm around Holly as they posed for Isabel.

Claire was in the habit of selling their life in Vermont to her friends who chose city living or high-powered careers. She met Michael when he was just finishing his Doctorate of Veterinary Medicine and she was studying nutritional sciences at Cornell. His specialty was large animals, and when an opportunity for him to purchase a practice in rural Vermont arose, he went for it, with her open-eyed and honest support. But it had been hard to find her place in the tight knit community, and slow going.

"You'll love it here," she added, as Isabel's camera whirred and clicked.

That night, Claire stayed up late making an angel food cake with a raspberry amaretto sauce. She used the last of the raspberries they'd picked and frozen in the fall. Michael came home just as she was folding in the egg whites and hugged her from behind. He'd been called to help birth triplet lambs at the Wilde's farm, and he smelled musky like blood. His cheek was cool on hers.

"This is the tricky part. So, don't jiggle me."

"You can multi-task. I know you can," Michael said, blowing in her ear.

"Stop!" But she smiled at their entwined reflection in the window in front of her. Claire carefully dipped her spatula in the fluffy batter and felt light herself - a stirring of lust for her husband, the scent of spring in the damp night air, the thought of delivering this cake as a welcome gift to Isabel and her family.

The next morning, Holly and Claire walked to Isabel's house and rang the bell. In the large front hall of the house, Isabel lifted the lid off the cake carrier. "Oh my God, Claire!" she cried and called to her husband. "Theo! Look at this confection! You have to come meet Claire—my new best friend—and her daughter Holly."

Isabel put her arm around Claire's shoulder and gave a squeeze. Theo, tall and thin with a neat brown beard, grinned as he came into the room.

"Isabel spoke rapturously about the pair of you," he said, holding out his hand. "Look at her, she's practically floating she's so happy."

"I am," Isabel said, winking at him. "Where's Darcy? Darcy, come downstairs!" As she leaned toward the stairway to yell, the cake tipped in her arm. Theo saved the cake with a quick hand.

"Oh my gosh; that would have been a disaster," Isabel said and batted her eyes at Theo. "He's my knight in shining armor. And, he's a scholar of Slavic languages, can you imagine? He can tell me he loves in me in seven languages. Oh there you are!"

Claire turned to see Darcy, who had quietly slipped down the stairs and into the front hall. Darcy was wearing a pink nightgown and fuzzy bunny slippers, and she snuggled up against her mother.

"Say hello to Holly, Darcy. This is the little girl I was telling you about; our new neighbors." Isabel used a hand to tilt Darcy's face toward her.

Claire could feel the hopeful tension in Holly's body in the pause that followed as the girls eyed each other.

"Do you want to help me unpack my stuffed animals? I have about a thousand," Darcy said, in a quiet little voice.

"Can I, Mom?" Holly tugged Claire's hand.

"Just for a bit, honey," Claire said and the girls were off up the stairs.

"Claire, that leaves us free for a ride, if you want to? Theo, don't eat the whole cake!" Isabel led Claire through the house toward the back door. On their way past the living room and dining room, Claire noticed the oriental rugs and warm cherry furniture, candlesticks with cream colored candles on the great fireplace mantel, and even a pile of magazines in a basket.

"I was so excited last night I couldn't sleep," Isabel said, waving her hand at her belongings.

Isabel rolled open the big barn door.

"What a difference a day makes," Claire said. Light flowed in the open door revealing the heads of three beautiful horses gazing at them from behind their stalls.

"We have lots of tack to put away and cleaning up to do, but aren't these living, breathing beings amazing?" Isabel strode over to a horse a color that reminded Claire of the chestnuts she used to collect in the fall. Isabel put her cheek against the horse's high shoulder.

"My husband—Michael—is a vet. He talks about the horses he takes care of like they are almost human. They are so expressive, I guess," Claire said, walking closer to a tawny colored horse. She let the horse sniff her.

"And empathetic," Isabel said. "I feel like they get me when no one else does. They get me without me having to explain anything."

"Nice to have that in one's life." Claire thought about last night when she and Michael finally got to bed and then together said *peepers!* and then both listened, rapt, at the first chorus from the first frogs of the spring. Claire remembered her first spring in Vermont, hearing the peepers. When Michael had said, "Looks like you made it through your first winter," she'd burst into tears.

"Indeed." Isabel stepped back and looked at Claire. "Are you up for a ride?"

"I'm not much of a horse person. If we went easy on the dirt roads, I'd be fine," Claire said touching the horse's soft nose. She liked the idea of horses, she supposed, more than the experience of horses.

"Well, then you take that baby nuzzling you. She's as sweet—and boring!– as can be. Darcy calls her Kathy because she couldn't say Café Au Lait!"

Isabel held Café steady while Claire, feeling ungraceful, clambered on. She watched Isabel around the horses and felt calmed, as the horses seemed to be. Isabel was easy, that's what she was. Claire breathed and tried to bring some of that ease into her own body. Thankfully, Café seemed as Isabel promised, boring, or bored.

On the road, Isabel exclaimed at the beauty of the red-winged blackbirds perched on the reeds surrounding the Peterson's pond down the hill. How do they do that? They stopped to admire the clear, green water spilling down Branch Brook. Isabel pointed to a wasp's nest from the previous summer, still dangling after a hard winter from a high limb of a maple tree.

"Look at that! Doesn't it look like it is only holding on by a thread?" Isabel asked.

"I've walked this road a hundred times this winter with the dog and never noticed that," Claire said, this realization astonishing her.

Isabel turned toward her. "So tell me about you, Claire. What do you notice? What do you do?"

What do you notice? An odd question and one that unsettled her, but also made her feel seen, dug into.

"I am a homemaker and a serial volunteer, and I've started a small catering and baking business. I sell cakes and cookies at some local shops, and I do wedding cakes, things like that. I'm toying with the idea of opening my own bakery." She told Isabel about moving to Vermont from Ithaca, about going with Michael on 'house' calls in the middle of the night before Holly was born, about her favorite flourless chocolate cake recipe. Isabel's interest and delight in everything gave Claire a sense of accomplishment that she often found elusive.

At the end of the road, they turned and started back. Nearing the Peterson's pond, Isabel urged her horse into a faster pace, calling over her shoulder, "I just can't help myself! We need to run!"

Claire clucked Café Au Lait into a little faster pace, but Isabel and her chestnut horse were up and over the hill and gone. Just then, Marcia Peterson, slowing down her red minivan to turn into her driveway, came to halt and when she pulled up beside Claire.

Marcia unrolled her window. "I was just passed by the most beautiful and speedy horse and rider and now I see you out here, too."

"Hey, Marcia. That was Isabel Bean. She and her husband and daughter just moved into the farm. This," Claire patted her horse on the head, "is Café Au Lait, and she and I are about the same speed, as you can see!" She could feel the cool air blowing from Marcia's air conditioning.

"I'd love to meet them. I need to get my ice cream home before it melts, but I'll stop in and welcome them to the neighborhood."

Claire remembered moving here two years ago on a hot summer day. Marcia and her husband had stopped by with homegrown tomatoes and cold beer.

"That's great. She'd loved that, I know." Café Au Lait started to amble forward.

"Okay then, have a nice ride, and call me when you want to walk the dogs," Marcia called as she pulled away.

Claire rolled down her car window and turned off the engine in the school parking lot. Mowers were whirring in the background somewhere, and the air smelled like cut grass. Claire watched from her parking spot as other mothers wandered toward the school entrance to pick up their kids. Something inside her tightened when she was here, waiting to scoop Holly up for piano lessons, watching other women gather in pairs and groups, easy with one another. It was a vague, long-ago playground memory of not belonging, of not quite knowing how to easily mingle. Not even a memory, just a feeling. She felt overwhelmed by the competence and confidence of all these women, by their accomplishments, by their seemingly endless ability to do it all and look fabulous, in an athletic and outdoorsy way. These were women who could organize in a crisis to support others with good deeds and hot dinners. But would any of them, she wondered, ever ask for help? Where were the cracks?

Isabel appeared at her window. In her arms was a large bundle of pussy willow and forsythia.

"I was hoping I'd see you here, Claire! These are for you; a thank you for the cake, the ride, your tips on where to get haircuts and teeth cleaned—etcetera, etcetera!" She thrust the bouquet through Claire's open window.

"It's gorgeous. Thank you, Isabel." Claire laid the bundle on her passenger seat and opened her door. "Shall we walk over and get the girls?"

Isabel linked her arm through Claire's. "This day is *killing* me. Stunning. I never noticed spring so intensely in the city. Maybe we should go on a hike or something tomorrow? Or shoe shopping first—I need hiking boots and sneakers."

"Let's do that. Shop and hike," Claire said as they walked across the playground arm in arm. She had two hundred cupcakes to bake for a wedding on Saturday, but that was four days away.

The next morning, Isabel knocked on the door just after the school bus pulled away. Claire and Michael had been drinking coffee with the crossword puzzle on the table between them. Claire glanced at the clock and went to the mudroom, which served as their entry way, where she saw Isabel on the stoop.

"Oh dear, I'm still in my bathrobe," Claire said, opening the door. Morning fog hung low in the hills. "But come in. Coffee?"

"Maybe I should have called, but I had an idea." Isabel pulled off her cowboy boots in the mudroom and followed Claire into the kitchen.

Claire introduced Isabel to Michael as she pulled a mug out of the cupboard.

"Welcome to the hill," Michael said, rising and holding out his hand.

"So nice to meet you. What luck to have you next door," Isabel said, shaking Michael's hand, in her two. Claire admired her beauty each time she saw her and wondered what Michael saw. She wished she wasn't wearing her purple fleece bathrobe.

"I just love Claire. She's been so welcoming," Isabel said as she walked toward the coffee pot.

"She's the best, that Claire," Michael said, putting down his coffee cup and checking his watch. "Gotta run. Talk to you later?" He gave Claire a soft kiss on the cheek, said, "A pleasure to meet you," to Isabel and went to the mudroom to get ready to leave.

Isabel took her coffee black.

"What's your idea, Isabel?"

"How about we go to Boston today? Shoe shopping? You know, hiking boots for me, mud boots, sneakers, all the country foot wear I need? And, we can get sandals for summer. Maybe get pedicures? I know there's not a whole lot of that going on up here."

"Boston?" Claire and Michael went to Boston for special events, the weekend, vacation; never to just go shopping.

"I'll drive! We'll be back by the time the school bus gets back. Pretty please?" Isabel clasped her hands together.

"I need to get started on two hundred cupcakes. I don't know, Isabel." Claire closed her eyes and thought about her to-do list.

"How about I help you with the cupcakes tonight or tomorrow?"

Claire was efficient with the baking, and had already bought the ingredients. There was nothing else she really needed to do today.

Claire opened her eyes. "Oh, what the heck!"

"Thank you, Claire! Michael was right. You *are* the best!" Isabel pulled the crossword puzzle toward her. "Okay. I'll work on this while you beautify."

Claire took the stairs two at a time, and from the upstairs window, she saw the fog disappearing, sharpening the tall trees around her house.

"I don't think I've ever seen you in shoes like that," Michael said. Claire looked down at the improbable sandals, high with intricate straps. Michael had two sets of boots, a pair of sneakers and his funeral shoes, as he called them.

"Shoes like what?" She continued slicing bread, hoping he would notice her freshly pedicured toes. "You don't like them?"

"I'm not saying I don't like them. They're actually quite sexy. But, can you walk?" Sometimes he was innocent and stupid and infuriatingly right.

"It is a little tricky." The shoes pinched right near her big toe.

"Are they new?" Michael walked to the fridge and pulled out a Long Trail.

"No. They're a gift from Isabel." And they were a gift, a token of Isabel's appreciation for Claire's willingness to be spontaneous that day. Claire had decided at some point during the day not to mention the road trip to Michael. Not to lie, of course, if he asked. But, if he didn't ask it just seemed simpler to not bring it up. She just wanted a little slice of something that was her own.

"Ah, Isabel."

"What does that mean?"

Michael took a piece of bread out from under the knife. "She's pretty high octane. I mean, I barely met her, but she's...tornadic...."

"Did you make up that word?" She scooped up the bread and placed it in a basket and turned to the vegetables steaming on the stove. *Click click.* She could hear her heels. Michael followed and came up behind her at the stove, putting his hands in her front pockets to pull her close.

"Tornadic. Tornado like, I think." He scratched his cheek on hers.

"You're ridiculous." Claire shrugged him off, and then turned to kiss his cheek. "She might have seemed that way this morning because she was all put together, had ideas for the day. I was still lounging around in my bathrobe with my bedhead."

"You were in your bathrobe? I never notice what you're wearing because I know you're naked underneath."

"Ha." Claire smiled, lifting the lid to the vegetables, letting the steam warm her face.

For the next three days, Claire buckled down and baked and frosted her gourmet cupcakes. Red velvet. Vanilla with a vanilla bean infused icing. Key lime. And her favorite, Devils Food with a mocha butter cream frosting. Claire didn't hear from Isabel or see her. She called her twice to see if she wanted to be a cupcake tester, but there was no answer, and Isabel didn't call her back. When Marcia called to see if she wanted to walk the dogs, she was up to her elbows in confectionary sugar and said no. Later, when Claire did walk Biscuit, she almost knocked on Isabel's door, but something in Isabel's noticeable absence the past days made her feel sad, even discarded, and she called Biscuit off their land and headed home. They'd had so much fun; Claire had sort of got it into her head that she see or talk to Isabel every day, that this is the kind of friendship they would have. Sister-like.

After delivering the cupcakes, Claire and Holly were passing the rainy Saturday sorting clothes and toys to give to Goodwill. The phone rang just after lunch.

"You are summoned to High Tea! Come at 3 p.m., bring Holly and plan on speaking in an accent of your choice!" Isabel seemed to have chosen a Scottish brogue of some sort.

"Sounds wonderful" Claire said, "I'll bring some leftover cupcakes."

"American accents don't count!" Isabel sang. "You have to do better than that, Claire."

It was still pouring when Claire and Holly ran over to the Beans' house. Claire carried a big pink umbrella over their heads, but the rain was coming sideways at them, and they arrived soaked. Isabel and Darcy met them in the big front hall, dressed in gowns and white gloves and bright red lipstick. Isabel wore a deep blue satin dress, strapless and elegant, with a single diamond on a chain around her neck.

"Apparently you don't know how to dress for high tea!" Isabel looked at them with her sparkling smile and beckoned them upstairs. Any fears that Isabel had tired of her vanished.

Holly followed Darcy, who looked more gleeful and childlike than Claire had ever seen her, into the playroom where a vast trunk overflowed with dress up clothes. Claire trailed Isabel into her closet, a room almost as big as Claire's master bedroom.

"Take that stuff off," Isabel said. The closet smelled of leather, and lavender, the crisp smell of dry cleaning. Claire was embarrassed; Isabel had such a beautiful figure, long limbed and elegant, enviously athletic looking but fleshy in the right places, as Michael had said of certain actresses. Claire fretted about the old bra she had on underneath. She was embarrassed about her pooching tummy and about her choice of underwear. The lack of places to shop in town, the comfort of a marriage, she'd kind of let things go. Isabel probably wore lacy things and thongs.

"Oh, hurry up, you silly. Pretend you're at the gym in the locker room with all the naked ladies." Isabel turned her back and flipped through the rack of dresses.

Claire did what Isabel said and slowly unbuttoned her damp blouse. She shrugged it off and then yanked down her jeans, wet from the cuffs to the knees from the rain. Isabel turned to her and Claire crossed her arms over her stomach, uncomfortable.

"Pretend we're sisters." Isabel said. With red lips pursed, Isabel rifled through her clothes while Claire stood unclothed and chilled in her underwear.

"Don't be modest," Isabel said in her Scottish voice, eying her up and down. "Life's too short, Claire. You're beautiful anyway, don't you know that?" How long since anyone besides Michael had seen her undressed or called her beautiful? She always told Michael to turn out the lights.

Isabel pulled out a forest green silk dress with spaghetti straps and a sheer little jacket.

"This will look fabulous on you. You have to take off that ancient bra."

"Isabel, that won't fit. I—"

"Shush! You're no fun!" Isabel stood with one hand on her hip, the other holding the hanger. She looked like a child, about to stomp her foot.

Claire reached out a hand to touch the fabric, smooth and cool under her fingertips. Her wedding dress felt like this, light but weighty at the same time. Something of substance.

"All right already." She quickly reached behind her and unhooked her Maidenform bra and dropped it to the floor. Isabel handed her the dress and she floated it over her head, eyes closed for a moment listening to the material sing past her ears.

The dress fit her. Isabel zipped it up and squeezed her shoulders, her hands in their white gloves soft on her skin. She almost thought Isabel would kiss her neck, the way Michael sometimes did when she asked him to zip her up.

"Beautiful! Okay, accessorize and meet us downstairs. And wear these gloves," Isabel said peeling them off her own hands, exposing her white wrists. Underneath the gold bangles on Isabel's left wrist, scars like the scrape of fork stood up on her smooth skin.

Isabel pushed her in front of her full length mirror, saying, "Look at yourself!" as she swooped out of the room, calling to the girls.

Claire couldn't look at herself. She pictured the soft pale insides of Isabel's marred wrists and felt a chill on the back of her neck, still damp from the rain. She remembered a moment in Boston when Isabel told her to pose with her shopping bags. The sun shone right in Claire's eyes. "Open your eyes!" Isabel had ordered and then positioned herself so that her shadow fell over Claire, blocking the sun.

Now, Claire raised her eyes to her own reflection. In Isabel's clothes, she looked unfamiliar to herself. She had an urge to pull off the green satin dress and return to her wet, Saturday clothes. She felt out of her depths and drawn to go deeper. *Play the game, Claire.* She pulled her barrette out and shook her hair. A pair of black stilettos lay on the floor next to a pair of cowboy boots. From a lacquered tray on Isabel's bureau she picked up a tube of lipstick. She swiped it on and looked at her reflection. Her own sultry pose embarrassed her, and she hurried out of the room.

That night when Michael came home, Claire was starting dinner.

He watched her as she stirred sour cream into the hamburger stroganoff with one hand and took a sip of wine from a glass in the other. "I like the look; the lipstick."

She saw the greasy red imprint on the rim of the glass.

"Isabel threw a tea party." She put the spoon on the counter and walked over to Michael and kissed him hard.

The school's May field day was held outside on the grassy lawn of the playground. It was a cool damp day, so Claire spread a plastic tarp on the ground to watch the festivities. She'd learned from past years to prepare for unseasonable cold or unseasonable heat. She slid new batteries into her camera and pulled on a sweater, waiting for the children to march out to the field and begin their bean bag tosses and tug-of-wars and potato sack races. Marcia Peterson shook out a plaid wool blanket next to her.

"Help yourself to coffee from the thermos, Claire," Marcia nodded her head toward the stainless steel container, propped between a video camera bag and an umbrella with yellow ducks on a blue background. Just before the kindergarten class started doing wheelbarrow races against the 5th graders, Isabel plopped down next to Claire. She wore sun glasses and pulled a tangerine out of her pocket and started peeling, tossing the rind onto the grass.

"This is a bit dull, don't you think? Will anyone notice if we leave?" she whispered in Claire's ear.

"What do you mean?" Claire could feel the cold seep up from the earth through the thin plastic.

"This thing is going to last forever," Isabel nodded toward the program in her lap. "Can you get up and snap a few pictures of all the kids? I found a great country diner that serves only organic food. I'm starved."

Claire looked at her; there was edginess in Isabel's voice and her knee bounced slightly.

"What're you looking at me like for? Come on you goody two shoes." Isabel looked tired, the skin around her eyes thin and bluish when she pushed her sunglasses to the top of her head.

"I want to stay."

"You don't really want to stay, do you? I mean we have years more of these things to look forward to." Isabel rolled her eyes. "You're afraid to leave, what people will think."

When Holly wasn't looking, when her class was setting up for an egg toss, they left. Claire held her head rigid, walked as if it was an emergency, feeling Marcia's curious eyes on her back.

Buckled into Isabel's black jeep, as it lurched out of the parking lot, Claire said, "Stop. You know what? I want to go back. I don't want to leave."

Isabel continued forward. "Party pooper! You came with me. No one held a gun to your head."

"Stop, Isabel. I mean it." Claire held on to the overhead handle, waiting for sudden movement, forward or back.

Isabel pulled to the curb with a hard turn and a quick stop. She folded her arms on the steering wheel and put her head down on her arms. Claire unbuckled, unsure what to do or say. She looked out the window at the gray day and looked back over her shoulder at the far away gathering of people in the school yard. Was Isabel crying? She thought of Isabel's tender wrists, the feel of Isabel's arm linked with hers. Claire felt afraid and that whatever choice she made now would be wrong.

"Okay," Claire said. "A quick bite to eat, but I need to be home by the time Holly gets off the bus." Claire slowly buckled herself back in, watching Isabel rise from her slump and put the car in gear.

"You *are* the best. But don't you always have fun with me?" Isabel put her blinker on and moved back onto the road, the edgy sharp Isabel replaced by some duller version of herself.

The school yard was empty and the buses had left by the time Isabel dropped Claire at her car. Claire slammed the door without saying goodbye, shutting in Isabel's words of apologies for getting them back late. But Isabel had dawdled over Boston Crème pie and a cup of coffee, even as Claire signaled for the check.

Holly had never before gotten off the bus to an empty house. Claire took the stretch of road up the hill fast, holding her body forward over the wheel, as if this would get her home sooner and erase her mistake of letting Isabel prod her into leaving the field day. The cat ran out before she saw it, too late. A thud vibrated under the car and she looked in horror at her rearview mirror.

"Oh, Christ." She pulled over and grabbed the box of tissues from passenger seat. The dust stirred up by her tires hung over the cat, splayed and still on the road. Claire knelt down, praying no one else would come by. Blood dribbled out of the cat's mouth. Claire poked the cat gently with her finger. She pulled out some tissues and carefully dragged the cat to the long grass edging the road. Michael would help her with the dead cat, bury it. Later.

Claire drove the rest of the way slowly, her thighs shaking and her scalp tingling with sweat.

Holly sat on the front steps. "Mom, did you see that Ollie and I won the egg toss?!"

"Wonderful, sweetie." She stood by the side of the car for a second, willing her heart to be quiet.

"Where were you, Mommy?" Holly's face pressed into her ribs so hard Claire felt like they might crack.

"Did you get lots of pictures? I want to show Daddy."

Claire washed her face in the bathroom then took the cloth and washed under her arms, too. Someone once said sweat from exertion smelled different than sweat from fear. In the bathroom mirror, Claire saw her own eyes and the skin around them bluish and tired, just like Isabel's had been today.

The sound of the basement door closing and Michael and Holly's voice twining together rose up the stairs. Then Michael called, "Where are you, Claire?"

"I'm up here." She dried her face and came out of the bathroom. Michael was pulling his undershirt over his head, and she was overwhelmed with gratefulness at the sight of him doing exactly what he always did.

"You don't want to come anywhere near me until I take a shower," Michael said. "It's been one of those days."

She went to her drawer and pulled out a sweater, watching him in the mirror over her bureau.

"I ran over a cat today, coming up the hill, and I just left it by the side of the road. Did you see it?" She felt unsettled, and wondered if confessing that she'd left the field day to Michael would make her feel better or worse. Michael would be judgmental, she decided, and she didn't need that on top of everything else today.

Summer was coming and with daylight lingering so long into the evenings, it was hard to get Holly to bed. After a family game of badminton, Michael escorted Holly to bed and returned to the deck with two cold beers, where Claire had lit citronella candles. They waited for the fireflies to start popping. Across the field, lights came on at the Bean's house—inside and out and even in the barn.

"They must have stock in the electric company," Michael said as they clinked their beer bottles together. "Do they ever sleep?"

She rolled the cold beer against her cheek and put her feet up on Michael's lap. "I don't think I've ever known anyone like her. I mean, she's got this energy and excitement, which I love." Intensity, she thought. Demanding.

"But?" He put his hand on her knee.

"She's just hard, sometimes. She likes to have her way, I guess."

"She's a different breed." Michael clinked his bottle against hers. "She reminds me of a high strung horse. The kind no one can ride, or break."

Claire thought about that. What about Theo? Had he broken her, so to speak, or just let her be? He was often off doing his research or writing in his office. What she witnessed, she supposed, is that he was hands off; he let her be herself.

"What kind of horse am I?" Claire asked. What kind of horse would Isabel say she was? What did she call Café au Lait? Sweet and boring.

"I have no clue." He pinched her toe.

"Really?"

"Don't you think sometimes the closer you get to someone the less clearly you see them?" Michael asked.

"God. That kind of question reminds me of us in grad school, getting high with you and your roommates." She remembered asking each other things like *what is the color blue, what do grapefruits have to do with grapes, and can you ever really know another person?* Of course, she could not remember their answers, but she certainly remembered sliding out of her chair because she had laughed so hard.

The fireflies started to sparkle and pop like a wave undulating over the field. The first summer they lived here, Michael took her outside just after dusk on a late June evening. *Thank you for moving here,* he whispered as they watched the light show.

"Let's do that again sometime," Michael said.

"Get high?"

"Laugh our heads off."

Claire looked at him as he looked out at the panoply of fireflies skittering over the field.

"We can't today," Claire said into the phone when Isabel hit her with a scheme to spend the day at a water park 100 miles away. "I am behind in so much; we're staying put." She had a wedding cake to complete and four dozen orange-ginger scones to make for a local coffee shop.

And she'd finally said yes to an invitation to have a picnic at Marcia Peterson's pond.

"Oh you're no fun. Come on."

Claire stood at her kitchen window, and through the leaves of the trees and over the grass of the field, she could make out Isabel's house. Where Isabel was pouting.

"We are having a picnic at Marcia's pond. I'm sure she won't mind if you and Darcy come, too." The words shot out of her mouth before she had a chance to think about it.

"I find Marcia sort of prissy. I think she judges me."

Claire ran hot water into the sink and swirled in soap. She plunged the coffee pot into the bubbles.

Claire and Marcia sat on little beach chairs on the sand by the edge of the water. Holly and Marcia's two children had waded out to a little dock and were lying on their stomachs watching the water. Claire could hear the tires of Isabel's red wagon bouncing on the gravel road before Isabel and Darcy rounded the driveway. The wagon got stuck in the sand and Claire was about to get up and lift an end when Isabel gave a sharp tug on the black handle of the red wagon and it tipped.

"Shit! Nothing is going right today." Isabel stood and watched as her cooler tumbled, the canvas bag with towels and sunscreen and shovels spilled, and a thermos rolled down toward the water.

Claire and Marcia collected Isabel's things and brushed off the sand. Slowly, Isabel unfolded her chairs. Darcy had wandered to the water's edge and stood knock-kneed and frail. Claire went to her and rubbed sun block on her shoulders.

"Is it broiling already or is it me?" Isabel said. As if a shade had been snapped up to let in sun, she was suddenly all action. She unzipped her cut-offs and pulled off her tank top to reveal a tiny black bikini with gold flecks that made Claire sharply aware of Marcia who wore a one-piece suit and a cover-up, and who'd confided in her about her attempts to diet, to get rid of the pounds that had gathered on her since child birth. Isabel ran after the children into the green water of the pond.

She emerged like some golden dripping goddess ready to hold court.

"I forgot glasses," Isabel said and dug in her canvas bag.

Marcia got up and went toward the house.

"Marcia?" Isabel yelled through cupped hands, "Bring limes! And a knife!"

"Say please, at least," Claire said.

"PLEASE!" Isabel yelled and then mouthed "mom" at Claire.

"I...just...you know...be nice." Claire wormed her toes into the warm sand.

"I am nice aren't I?" Isabel's voice sounded mocking, but when Claire looked at her, her eyes were strangely earnest.

Marcia returned with a stack of plastic cups, two limes, a small knife and a cutting board. "Just what do you have planned for us anyway?" she asked.

"Oh, something to make a day in the sun a party!" Isabel expertly cut the limes, wiped them on the rims of three cups, put the rims of the cups into a small plastic container of salt, and filled the cups from her thermos.

"Bottoms up girls!" Isabel took a long drink.

Claire got a head rush from just sniffing the Margarita. She stuck her tongue in to taste the sharpness as Isabel stared at her. Marcia glanced at her watch and took a polite sip before setting the cup down in the sand. Claire gave Marcia a little eye roll and lifted her cup to Isabel's before drinking.

Later, as Claire felt woozy from drinking and baking in the sun, Marcia drove Claire and Holly home. On the way, Claire thought she might get sick and rolled down the window.

"Do you need help getting in Claire?" Marcia's voice was cold. Claire felt sick hearing the edge in Marcia's voice. Holly was looking at Claire the way Darcy sometimes looked at Isabel.

"We're okay." Claire gathered her bag and towels and shut the car door, thinking, *please don't be such a prig, Marcia.* Inside, she got a drink of water and then lay on the living room couch in her damp bathing suit. The room was moving. The volume of the TV thunderous. She thought maybe she should get a bowl. She had a vision of Isabel. A life-size spark, lighting things up. And then a vision of herself. A dry pile of hay, ready to burn.

Michael's hand on her leg woke her. The dusky half-light graying the windows disoriented her.

Had someone driven nails through her temples? "Oh, God, is it morning?" Michael seemed very tall, standing above her. Holly walked in eating an ice cream sandwich and Claire felt in no position to tell her no food in the living room.

"Hol," Michael's voice was gentle and he put his hands on Holly's shoulders and pointed her toward the kitchen. "And, then bed, when you finish that," he called after her.

Claire pushed herself up to sitting and felt the tequila still vibrating through her body.

"We were at the pond and Isabel was acting so weird." Each word was like a little mallet striking the middle of her brain. "And then she made margaritas. It was totally stupid of me to drink…. Way too much. I don't know…."

She could see Michael's bare feet. Say something, she thought. His silence was the worst.

"Well, we're lucky right? Kids are okay. Everyone is okay." His voice was tight.

She nodded, and a wave of nausea rippled through her.

"Claire," Michael knelt down in front of her. "To be completely honest, I don't know whether to be madder than hell or to feel sorry for you."

"Don't feel sorry for me." No one should feel sorry for her, not Marcia, not Michael, not Isabel. No. You make your bed, and you lie in it.

"Not about how you are feeling this minute. But why you've gotten so sucked in by Isabel."

"God. All of you stop blaming Isabel. Blame me if you want to blame somebody." She pulled a sofa cushion over her head but kept her eyes on his feet until he walked away.

She hadn't seen Isabel for a few days, not even her black Jeep zipping up and down the road. She stood outside by the grill on the deck and looked out over the field, through the trees, to Isabel's house and barn, holding a plate while Michael slipped hamburgers onto it from the grill. She needed to talk to her.

After dinner, Claire walked over to the Bean's house. The horses were out in the field, heads down, biting off blades of grass and chewing in that slantwise motion. Isabel sat on her deck, perfectly still, dressed in a deep purple blouse, her hair pulled into a tight little ponytail. Claire, even through her anger, could see beauty; the sharpness of Isabel and the soft mountains, violet shadows resting in the hollows and dark clouds moving in, deepening the contrast.

"Isabel," Claire called, sorry the risers under her feet didn't creak her arrival. She wanted to crack the still air around Isabel.

"Isabel," she said again.

Claire moved in front of Isabel. Isabel's face was slack and heavy and her eyes, usually so full of shine, had gone dull under heavy lids. "Christ," Claire said and knelt before Isabel.

"Are you...? Okay?" Claire put her hand on top of Isabel's, but Isabel didn't meet her eyes. She was looking out at some far unfocused place. The crackle of energy that usually pulsed from her was replaced by a heavy despondency. It frightened Claire.

"What's up, Isabel?" Claire's fingers drummed on top of the cool hand under hers.

Isabel slowly turned her hand until she and Claire were palm to palm.

"You're so much better than I am." Isabel's voice was low. Claire pulled her hand away from Isabel's and stood up, stunned.

"Oh, come on."

"You are, Claire. Remember what I said when I first met you? I always wanted a neighbor like you." Isabel raised her eyes.

"Stop it," Claire said. The wind blew, smelling of rain moving in and sweet late August phlox. "I was annoyed by the stuff you pulled at the pond, but I am not better than you, and I never—"

"You are so *normal*." Isabel gave a laugh, but it was hard and edgy.

"Maybe. Predictable. But not better." Sweet and boring, she thought.

"Do you know you have everything and are everything I've always wanted?" Isabel's arms lay limply on the arms of her chair but the cords on her thin neck stood in relief under her smooth skin.

"I don't know what you're talking about," Claire said. "Now you. *You* are something else and I...love it." It was true and not true, but it was what Claire needed to say.

"You have no edges," Isabel said. "But I feel jagged and ugly and so jittery I want to pop out of this skin and other times so tired. Oh God. Just go home, Claire." Isabel leaned forward, face in her hands. Her hair fell away and Claire saw the white nape of her neck.

"Is Theo home? Can we go inside and make some tea?" Claire did not want to be alone with this.

"No. No." Isabel stood up. The cool dusk crept up from the grass and the colors—the bright purple of Isabel's blouse, their fractured reflections in the panes of the house, the planters of begonias at the edges of the deck—pulsed vibrantly and Claire felt very alive, sharply aware as if she was watching this all in slow motion. This is how Isabel made her feel.

Claire remembered a moment at their tea party when Isabel set the teapot down after pouring for all of them. She put her hands in front of her as if in prayer and looked at Holly, Darcy, and then her. She knew, Claire thought. She knew I saw. *I should have asked her.*

"How can I help you, Isabel?" Isabel got up and slowly walked across the deck, and then slipped into the house, shutting the door behind her. Claire waited a moment, not sure whether to follow. She saw Theo at the kitchen window, looking out at her. She began to walk toward the door, but he shook his head and pulled the shade.

The wind was up now. Claire stepped off the deck into the grass. Grumbles of thunder had the horses ears up, their big jaws stilled. She would put them in the barn for the night, before the storm. She could do that for Isabel, Claire thought, climbing over the fence.

Sanctuary Therapy

Moondog tugs my hand.

"Let's go down to the barn Mom, to see what they do when we're not looking," he says.

He's stalling on bedtime, which I just announced; plus he seems to believe—or wants to believe—that the animals chat with one another when we're not looking. Moondog's real name is Jackson. He gave himself the name Moondog one night when he howled at the moon along with our golden retriever, Hilda. The dog spent today in the woods with Nick while Nick downed trees that splintered in the last ice storm. Hilda's given into exhaustion and is curled on her bed next to the woodstove.

"Socks? Long underwear? And find your hat," I say, seeing the stars through the diamond shaped window at the top of the stairs. Clear and cold. I can hear Nick's saw in the basement, as if he thinks he can build himself—us—a way out. Building is his prayer.

Today Moondog had tube after tube of blood drawn, to see how his first round of chemo went and to check his kidney and liver function. Functions we take for granted. I called Nick from the bathroom at the hospital. I could hear the wind in the trees where he was. Yes, of course, he said, he'd come to see Dr. Bradley with me tomorrow to discuss results. But, it gets so complicated. Why do I need to ask? Why was he in the woods when I was in a stall in the ladies room?

"Bundle up, buster," I say, stabbed by the normalcy of this exchange. Moondog crosses his eyes, which sometimes softens me. His eyes are so big, hazel with darker flecks, and I am exposed to every pain, every needle, every indignity inflicted on him, every time I look into them.

I open the basement door and listen. It's quiet.

"Nicky? We're going out to the barn before bed."

"To see what they do when we're not looking," Moondog calls under my arm. If I could catch Nick's eye right now, we might wink at each other, knowing what animals do in the dark, whether we're looking or not. We need a laugh.

"I haven't shoveled the front steps," Nick shouts up the stairs.

"We'll be careful." I am so full of care that I crawl into bed every night quivering with exhaustion from being so careful. Every step, every wince, every bite Moondog takes, I am there. Nick takes care of us by fortifying railings, de-icing steps, and cleaning up the bathroom when Moondog gets sick.

Nick restores old homes, taking them down to bare bones when necessary. He has never thrown up his hands and said, Can't do it. Never, about anything. When he can't fix something, well, I don't know. I've never seen him not fix something.

Outside, everything is traced in snow; the rooster weathervane permanently rusted toward north, the roof of the barn, every twig, every leaf that hasn't fallen, the white lights Nick wrapped around the tallest pine he could manage to climb. On the slick steps, I reach my hand out, ready to catch Moondog. Sometimes I think I am going to shatter like a windshield but not fall out. Safety glass. People will see me from afar and say, 'Oh, look how well she's holding up.'

Moondog tugs his elbow away from my gloved hand.

"Look at Orion," I say. The sky is brilliant and the air sharp as knives on my bare cheek. The basement windows throw tongues of light.

"Shh. We're trying to sneak up, Mom."

Moondog presses his eye to a crack in the barn door.

"What do you see, babe?"

"Same old same old." He is truly disappointed.

Goddamn animals talk. Just once. Please.

My mother comes the next morning so that Nick and I can go see Dr. Bradley. In one arm, she holds a Trader Joe's bag and in the other, an enormous stuffed Saint Bernard. She whispers, "Emily, let me and Dad give you money to take Jackson to Disney World." This is so make-a-wish that I panic and think she must know something that only Dr. Bradley or God can know.

Nick is chipping away at the ice on the steps where the salt he sprinkled has burned holes. I wait until he's done and step down carefully. I've put on leather boots with two-inch heels not meant for this weather. Going to the hospital reminds me of flying: if you dress up, you have a better chance of being bumped to first class. You get more respect.

In the waiting room of the pediatric oncology clinic, we are the only adults without a child. My mother is probably making Moondog chocolate chip pancakes upon which she will swirl mountains of whipped cream. A little girl, maybe five, lies across her mother's lap. The mother presses her lips to the child's hat. I think she's lost her hair. I look down at the pearly buttons on my blouse before the girl catches me staring at her. Nick leans his elbows on his knees and puts his chin in his hands. He sits back and crosses his arms. He takes his glasses up to the light and cleans them with a corner of his shirt. I want to hold Nick's hand. I want Nick to take my hand. Sometimes I feel like the mere touch of him will let loose an unstoppable journey—free fall—into utter darkness. I can feel my anxiety start to gather itself like a tornado, honing in on why isn't Nick reaching for my hand. I wish I had Moondog on my lap to hold and smell and hold and hold. Somewhere I hear a child cry. I cross my legs and look at my boots, hoping they will make me feel as sharp and invincible as they look. There is a thin line of salt veering over the black leather, and I wet my thumb and rub.

The first time we met Dr. Bradley, I thought he was as good looking as any doctor on ER. Today there is a dab of shaving cream on his left ear and some crumbs on his balloon-dotted tie. On the hooks behind the door where Nick and I hang our coats, I see his brown winter coat with ski tickets hanging from the zipper and a homemade knit hat. I am momentarily shocked he has a life outside of saving my son.

Nick and I bump shoulders as we turn back and take the seats in front of Dr. Bradley. His square hands are laid flat on the papers covering his desk.

"Thanks for coming in."

Are there parents who don't?

"Look. Let's get right to it. We're getting there."

"But we're not there yet - ?" I cannot finish my sentence. Nick is looking at me.

"I'm pleased though. Let's go through it step by step."

I try to listen. His words flow over me. *White cell count over 20,000... induction stage goal is to put Jackson in remission...weekly administrations of vincristine for three to four weeks....* The voice inside my own head is shouting, "Just say he'll live." I watch Dr. Bradley's mouth move and watch Nick's head nodding. It's good he's nodding, right? The first time we sat here it looked like he was being eviscerated.

"...so what I'm thinking..." Dr. Bradley says.

I stare into Dr. Bradley's left eye, which is blue.

"...is that we will add CNS sanctuary therapy."

Sanctuary therapy? I picture Nick and myself down on our knees in the chapel near the elevators on the 4th floor, just past the nursing station. This cannot be what he means.

"What is that?" I say, pressing my palms together. Here's the church and here's the steeple. "We're not as smart as we look." If I keep things light and Dr. Bradley laughing, maybe he will say it's been one big joke.

"Central Nervous System," Nick quickly says. He's reading everything he gets his hands on, building his knowledge like he builds houses to withstand all forces of nature.

"Yes." Dr. Bradley seems relieved and turns to Nick. "CNS therapy will kill any cancer cells that might be hiding in the brain or spinal cord. Before this kind of therapy, close to 80% of patients relapsed with leukemic meningitis. This is a major therapeutic advancement."

He pauses. "Do you have any questions?"

Hiding in the brain or spinal cord?

I can feel Nick's eyes on me. I give him my *I'm fine* smile, the one I keep in my back pocket to plaster on my face when it feels like my face is going to dissolve and take me with it. On our way out, Dr. Bradley touches my shoulder. "This is a tough time. But it's going to be okay."

In the bathroom, I slide the lock on the stall door. I don't want anyone who doesn't know me to see me in such pain. I don't want people who know me—Nick—to see me either. What does Dr. Bradley mean, it will be okay? Is it about the facts or is it something more mystical—that we're all okay in the end?

I want to ask Dr. Bradley, "Will he be cured? Will he never feel pain? Should I pray? Do you believe in prayer or the power of positive thinking? You know those studies where it shows people live longer when they're being prayed for, even if they don't know they're being prayed for? What if you pray and you don't really believe? Have they done studies on that?" Sometimes I vomit after Moondog goes to bed. It's like everything I've held in all day needs to come out. I stand over the toilet.

When we're back in the truck, Nick asks, "Em, are you all right?"

I look at the spitting snow outside the window. "I'm still fighting how wrong this is, how unfair."

"What I heard made me hopeful." Nick puts the truck in reverse but keeps his foot on the brake.

Hopeful? Hopeful is for good weather and awaited phone calls. Hopeful is about luck and chance and things you cannot control.

"Say something, Emily."

I know him well enough to know that, tough man though he may be, I am his emotional barometer. He wants me to say I'm hopeful. He can go low on his own, but he can't ride the high if I'm not there.

We start to slowly move. Behind us the hospital disappears.

"I don't know how to live with this," I say. He moves his hand to my knee.

Nick drops me off and goes to work. My mother and Moondog are floating a tea towel over a bowl of bread dough. The warm kitchen smells yeasty. I toe off my boots by the door. I try to hug Moondog the way I used to hug him, when I was sure there would be thousands more. Otherwise, I might frighten him.

My mother follows me upstairs while I change. I list the facts and add, "Dr. Bradley says things look very good." It is impossible to look her in the eye. She doesn't push, just says, "I knew it, Em. I knew it."

Moondog has pulled the living room couch into the middle of the floor, near to the matching arm chairs. The whole contraption is layered with sheets and blankets. I get down on my knees to find a way in.

He's piled the place with pillows and is snuggled up with Hilda and his new stuffed Saint Bernard. The real dog has a resigned look, pointy snout resting on her paws. I crawl in.

"I need to pee and get a snack. Can you make sure Hilda doesn't leave?"

"I'll try," I say, carving out a spot for myself. "But you know Hilda, she'd rather be with you than anyone." He slips out, and I hear him padding around whistling and snapping, something he has just learned to do. It is so comfortable and warm. I lay on my back with my head on the Saint Bernard. The toilet flushes. I hear rustling in the kitchen.

Moondog has rigged up a flashlight from the ceiling. I reach up and turn it on. The place glows. Hilda opens her eyes and sighs and rolls, assuming the position of contentment once again.

Maybe we can all sleep in here tonight. Nick will curl around me, and I will curl around Moondog Jackson Hewitt, and he will curl around the dogs—real and saintly. We will all breathe in unison. We will be warm bodies in this dark den, all night.

The Last and Kindest Thing

Banjo could hardly walk anymore. Adam scooped him up to carry him outside to pee, no easy feat with Adam's bad back and Banjo being a 95-pound Bernese mountain dog. What had started as a limp in Banjo's back left leg had become an immobilization. The cancer in his bones had spread to his lungs. He lay down on his side in the yard. Banjo was suffering, failing more each day.

Marianne came outside, zipping her blue down parka.

"Do you think it's the humane thing to do, put him down?" Adam asked her as she fished for her keys in her jacket.

Marianne nodded slowly. "I think it's time."

She looped her arm through his, and they looked at Banjo lying flat on the brown grass. November wind cut through Adam's flannel shirt. For weeks they'd been talking, knowing this day was coming.

"Dr. Peterson said just to call when Banjo couldn't take it anymore." He'd call today. They'd do it today. Poor boy. Poor old boy.

"I'd come with you, but I'm worried about asking for a day off so soon," Marianne said. Marianne had just gotten the job detailing the insides of cars at A Clean Getaway. They needed the money; it was a struggle to keep up with the mortgage payments right now, and if they lost the house, he'd never get to see his daughter, Lily. If she wanted to visit, that is. If Esme ever let her. Going alone was okay. If Marianne came, Adam would end up worrying about her, comforting her. It would just be different. Sometimes it was easier to do these things yourself.

"I'm fine going by myself," he said.

"Goodbye sweet dog." Marianne squatted nose to nose with Banjo, tears slipping out her eyes. "I can't lose it now," Marianne said and ran out to her car so she wouldn't be late.

Slowly, Adam carried Banjo to the truck. Banjo lay on the towel Adam had placed on the front seat. Adam put his rig in reverse, stopping at the mailbox at the bottom of the driveway to pick up the inevitable stack of daily bills. He stuffed them into the glove compartment and touched Banjo's soft head. So many potholes on the dirt road to avoid. Adam had unrolled Banjo's window, and Banjo had his big snout resting on the frame. Look at him. It was almost as if the years washed away. Could Banjo know he was sniffing the murky pine woods for the last time, catching a little breeze up his nostrils causing him to sneeze? And how long had it been since Adam had really noticed the slow metronome of Banjo's tail against thigh?

Adam turned left on the main road, speed limit 40. He didn't want to go that fast. How slow could he go without someone honking at him? Adam drove by the church with the sandwich board outside announcing a corned beef supper, the general store where the boys pumping gas always gave Banjo a dog biscuit, the farm stand closed for the season, a field with gaggle of Canada geese making a rest stop on their way south. The red minivan tailing him gave a honk.

The geese waved up and away in a flawless take off. Adam squinted into the rearview mirror. What's the hurry, lady?

Up around the next curve, he put on his right blinker and slowed to turn into the parking lot of All Creatures Great and Small. The minivan sped by. Adam almost parked in the handicapped spot to make it easier on Banjo. Instead, he went to the far corner of the lot. He was going to have to carry Banjo anyway. This way, he'd have Banjo's warm breathing body in his arms for as long as possible.

"Come on, Pup." Adam opened the truck door and scooched his arms under Banjo's haunches. Banjo was too compliant. Adam wished he'd dig his feet into the seat, show some fight. Banjo whimpered as they walked, and Adam tried to shift how he was carrying him.

The receptionist, Ingrid, saw him at the door and came to hold it open. Inside the waiting area was bright and cheery. A mother and her young daughter sat in a pair of chairs, with a cat carrier containing a gray kitten perched across their knees. The walls were adorned with the usual posters of dogs with shiny coats, a yellow lab leaping in the sunshine to catch a Frisbee, a picture of a sleek cat curled on a child's lap. All the good things in life that always seemed slightly out of reach, or fleeting. Fleeting, that's more what he meant. Gone too soon. Adam put his nose into Banjo's fur. The mother looked at him with his big dog gathered in his arms. What a sight they must be. The vet tech, his name tag said Gabe, entered from behind the swinging doors and said quietly, "We can go this way." He'd been so sure that this was the right time—that this was the last and kindest thing he could do for his dog.

As the doors swung shut behind him, uncertainty halted him. Gabe put a hand on his elbow and just stood there for a second as Adam took a couple deep breaths, Banjo's fur tickling his nose. Who was he to decide when it was time for Banjo or any other living creature to leave his body behind? Adam thought his knees might buckle and the antiseptic odor mingling with the musk of animal didn't help. Banjo huffed in his ear. What Banjo? What? That Gabe had matched his pace to Adam's, had stopped dead in the hall in with him, and now the keening of Banjo in his, ear strengthened Adam's resolve—*his knowing*—and they began to move as one again down the hall into a back room.

Banjo sunk onto the paper covered steel table, his tags clinking against the metal. Dr. Peterson came in and laid a hand on Banjo's broad head and reached out the other hand to Adam.

"We're never ready, are we?" He murmured this as much to himself as to Adam, it seemed.

Adam circled his arms around Banjo's broad chest and laid his head against his shoulder. His fur felt thin now, but still warm, against Adam's cheek. Adam wanted to be as close to Banjo as possible. Fur. Skin. Muscle. Blood. Bone. The blue rivulets of veins, the apple-sized heart pumping mysteriously and continuously until it didn't anymore. Adam did not want Banjo to be alone, feel alone, when that happened. Maybe he should whisper a prayer in his ear.

Dr. Peterson slipped the IV in and released the anesthetic. Banjo twitched. Then, his body seized and his head reared. Banjo's jaw gnashed and snapped, his teeth piercing Adam's hand. Adam sprung back in confusion and boiling hot pain. Blood spurted from the punctures. Holding his hand up in front of his face, watching the blood pulse out, Adam's vision tunneled, his head twirled and all words disappeared. Dr. Peterson reached back and turned the door knob to throw open the door.

"Gabe! Towels!"

Gabe sped in and tightly wound a towel around Adam's shaking bloody hand.

"Banjo?" Adam whispered into the clamor and confusion in the room.

Banjo was still.

He'd missed it.

Banjo's teeth had made three punctures in the index finger and palm of his right hand. No, no, he insisted when Dr. Peterson implored him, he wouldn't go to the hospital. It wasn't so bad. Dr. Peterson disagreed, called Gabe into drive him. No, Adam, insisted. He would go home, get Marianne, she would drive him. He thought about the fact they had no health insurance. No one was to worry. Please. He was fine. *He'd missed it.*

The waiting room was empty now. Murky November light barely made it over the windowsills. Everything had moved so fast.

"I'll just sit down for a second," Adam said to no one. Adam put his head down between his knees. The day was here then gone. Banjo was here then gone.

Ingrid emerged from the swinging doors with a glass of water.

"Thank you." He gulped it down, feeling the water cool his brain a little bit.

"How's the hand?" Ingrid went to her desk, back behind her counter, and moved some things around. Sticky notes. A jar of pens. He'd made a scene. They'd made a scene.

"Fine. I'm fine." The finger wasn't bad enough to merit medical bills. He stood up slowly and put the glass on the counter in front of Ingrid.

Marianne was shocked about the finger and wanted details, a timeline, which he couldn't seem to give her. She'd been waiting by the front window for him, like Banjo did. Used to do. He didn't want to talk much about it; it was like time was a big ball of twine and he couldn't untangle it. Did the red minivan honk at him on the way home, as he drove carefully and slowly, his left hand throbbing in his lap? Did Banjo see the Canada geese shoot out of that field or did Adam alone see them on the return trip?

That night, Marianne spooned him in bed, her damp face between his shoulder blades until she fell asleep and let go. He couldn't cry. The pain in his finger and palm was real. But the whole event seemed like a movie he was watching replay in his head—some overly dramatic scene he was witnessing and starring in. *What happened?* Dr. Peterson explained that involuntary movements—seizures, vomiting, biting—occasionally happened during euthanasia; it was unpredictable. Maybe it was Banjo's big F-you.

Adam lay on his back and stared up at the brush stroke of moonlight illuminating the water stains from last winter's leaky roof. An ice dam had built up. Adam used the ladder to get up on the roof and sprinkle salt and break up the dam with an ice pick. But he'd never gotten around to fixing the cosmetic damage to the ceiling. Marianne had bugged him for a while last spring, but he'd been busy with some odd construction and auto repair jobs and would only remember when he lay down at night to sleep. He'd paint it this week, before Thanksgiving, before the snow came. He thought of the bills he'd stuffed into the glove compartment earlier today. There was one from the mortgage company; they just had to keep this house. He pushed himself up to look at the clock. 3:04 a.m.

Marianne turned in her sleep away from him, her mouth open and easy as she moved; all tension gone. Adam lifted the blankets and put his feet on the cold wood floor. He reached back with his uninjured hand to tug the blanket up over Marianne's shoulders.

In the living room, the luminescent November moonlight shimmered on the empty dog bed. He'd forgotten for a second why he felt such heaviness; the empty bed made his stomach hollow out. Oh. He stared at the bed then walked to the computer on the desk in the corner of the room and jabbed the power button. He stood right in the path of the moonlight, his white t-shirt glowing. Goddamn the pulsing hot ache of his finger. He wanted to feel it straight in his heart.

He sat down at the computer to type his weekly letter to Lily. Sometimes he enclosed money for her to spend on whatever 15-year old girls liked to spend their money on. He always paid his child support on time; that was one payment he wouldn't put off, not even now. Esme never acknowledged the money, and Lily never wrote him back. Someday he'd hear back from them. He was a different person—in a way different place—than he was when things were falling apart with Esme. He laid his wounded hand on the table, palm up so he could see Lily's name tattooed on his inner wrist, dark blue and always there. *Dear Lily,* he typed with his one good index finger.

The floor boards creaked behind him and Marianne tip toed out in her t-shirt.

"What're you doing? Are you okay?"

Ctrl Alt Del. The screen went black.

Adam swiveled in the chair. "I couldn't sleep," he said standing up. "Let's go back to bed." Lily wasn't a secret, but his weekly notes to her were. When Lily wrote him back, Marianne would be the first to know.

* * *

It had been a hell of a week with the finger, dousing it with water and antiseptic to keep it clean, laying his hand across Marianne's lap each morning for her to re-bandage it before she left for work, prodding the finger to see if it still hurt and how much. Adam had to turn down two auto repair jobs and an offer from his neighbor to split and stack five cords of wood. It killed him to say no.

"How does it feel today?" Marianne asked this morning, a gray rainy day, three days before Thanksgiving. She lifted his hand gently from the kitchen table. "I have to say it's still pretty red looking. More swollen, too?" she said, rewrapping it with white gauze and securing it with medical tape. Her hands didn't look so good either; dry and chapped from scrubbing the inside of cars.

"It doesn't hurt as much, I don't think." That wasn't exactly true, and it was beginning to bother Adam how tender it still felt, achy deep down to the bone. He flexed his fingers to reassure her. "Yeah. I think it's better." With his other hand, he lifted his cup of coffee to his mouth.

Marianne ran her fingers through her brown hair and snapped a barrette around a pony tail. "I'm giving you until Thanksgiving, Adam. If it's not better—like much better," she said slipping on her winter coat, "we're going to see the doctor."

"Okay," he said watching her walk into the kitchen to shake some ibuprofen into her palm. She downed it with the last of her coffee. She never complained. He stuck his hand out.

"Aren't we a pair?" Marianne asked, dropping three in his palm.

After she left, Adam went out to the truck and opened the glove compartment, where he'd been stuffing the bills. The towel he'd put on the seat for Banjo was still there. He picked up the towel and smelled it, catching the faint scent of his dog. Then he gathered up all the envelopes—Green Mountain Power, US Bank, Mountain View Gas and Oil, All Creatures Great and Small. Back inside, Adam cleared the coffee cups and cereal bowls off the kitchen table and began to lay out all the bills, one by one until they covered the whole table.

He took out his check book and began writing small checks. Then he wrote a note to go with each one. *Dear Sirs, in lieu of full payment this month, please accept this check as an indication of our intention to fully repay you when our employment status improves....* The phone rang, and he ignored it, listening as his neighbor left a message, "It's Ron again. I know it's not a lot of work, but I could use some help with the wood still. When you're back to being two-handed, give me a call, Adam."

Adam looked out the window, to the winter-stripped woods between their place and Ron's house, where their other dog, Humphrey, was buried. *They could not lose this house.* When Humphrey had been old and nearly blind, he'd stepped in a neighbor's trap of some sort, and was just about dead when Adam found him. The kindest thing he could do was shoot him. Then, he and Marianne built a cairn, just out of the rocks that came out of the hole they were digging, but it made a nice little tower.

Adam's hand throbbed in his lap. Thump thump thump, with each squeeze of his heart.

Marianne pulled the turkey breast for their Thanksgiving dinner out of the oven and called to Adam to come eat. Adam heard her voice and smelled the buttery salty bird but could not, *could not*, get off the couch. Beyond the cloud of heat shimmering off of him, crowds cheered. A touchdown. His hand, lying mummified in white gauze on his stomach, felt as big as the pillow under his head. Did it even belong to him? It almost looked like someone else's body part that had been blown off and landed on him. But Lily's name was there. He held up his hand. Red lines raked from underneath the bandage, straight through Lily's name and under his shirt sleeve. The blood in his temples throbbed in time with the marching band on the TV. Did he scratch himself? Scrape his arm against something ragged?

"*Marianne?*" He didn't want to ruin Thanksgiving and all the work she put into everything, but he couldn't keep up the charade now.

Rushing in, Marianne tripped over the dog bed and knelt down beside him. Her forehead was damp from the steam from the potatoes she was mashing; the masher was in her hands and her flowered apron was dotted with bits of potato.

"What is it, sweetie?" Her voice was tight; she once told him worry made her throat feel all closed up.

He held up his arm and she took it and pushed up his shirt sleeve.

"What is this? Infection? Goddamn you for not seeing the doctor sooner!" She put a palm against his forehead. "You're hot. We're going to the hospital."

Marianne quickly untied her apron and tossed it on the couch. She sped into the kitchen and he heard the sound of the oven door open and closing. Adam tipped himself up to a sitting position and closed his eyes. He felt Marianne drape a blanket over his shoulders.

"Take my arm, Adam. Let's go. Are you steady enough?"

They intertwined arms, and he let himself be led to the truck, a hot buzzing around him, as if bees were hovering over him. He laid his head against the back of the seat and closed his eyes. He felt sweaty *and* cold and pulled the blanket closer and unrolled the window. Shivering and sweating, Adam let the piney breeze coming in the window wash over him. Marianne gunned it when they got to the main road. He opened his eyes and saw empty streets. Thanksgiving. Had he slept the rest of the way? He was aware of the speed of the car and the wind and of Marianne clearing her throat as she drove, but for a time he thought they were on a plane and then a subway in a tunnel underground, whooshing through the darkness, bells dinging as they arrived in a bright station.

It was the driver's side door ajar while the truck was running that caused the dinging, Adam realized when he heard Marianne say, "Here he is. I think we need help getting him into the wheelchair." He opened his eyes. There was a man in green, and a wheelchair, and Marianne, and the hospital soaring—all gleaming white and chrome and glass—behind them. Don't take my finger! A searing energy revved inside him and he felt stapled to the seat. Did he *whimper*? Did he whisper *no*? He wanted to go home. They would take his finger and charge him thousands of dollars. *All creatures great and small.* The man in the green gently took his elbow and guided him out of the truck. Adam's legs trembled but the man held him firmly and sat him down in the chair, placing his feet on the little metal pedals.

"I'll be right in," Marianne called to him as the man wheeled him away. "I just need to park the truck."

The man pushed him through air that cooled his clammy skin, in through doors that opened on their own, all with reckless rattling speed. Adam thought he saw the lady with the cat carrier or her knees, or no it was a striped pocketbook, with handles. Nearby a kid with his pant leg sliced and a bag of ice taped to his knee looked Adam up and down when he wheeled by. An older man slept splayed out on a chair next to a white haired lady with a coat on over her pink nightgown, her arms and wrapped around her own belly. Someone was plinking coins into the vending machine in the corner.

He was pulled backwards through another set of double doors. *Sorry* he thought he should say to the waiters still waiting, all watching him disappear. The red hot pain in his finger rippled from one point and pinged around in him like a pinball, sparking pain at every joint, each fingertip, even coated the inside of his eyelids.

Inside the curtained cubicle, he lay down on a bed. Cool hands touched his face and wrists. Warm hands spread blankets over his shivering body. Marianne whispered, "I'm here" in his ear. Then came the sweetest moment of pure elation before it all went dark.

His hand felt bloodless, cold. In the glow coming in through the window and the little stream of light coming in from the hallway, he saw his hand hanging above his head like a marionette. Rigged up and bandaged so that he couldn't inspect it. An IV attached to his other forearm dripped in cold fluid through a tube from a big bag hanging on the metal pole. He tried to wiggle his finger. Did it move or not? Did he still have it? Did he have the Goddamn finger? He tried to re-member. The truck ride and Marianne crying and the wheelchair and the boy with ice on his knee and a room and a needle and after that a black moment, like liquid chocolate melting over him—morphine? Where was Marianne? Where was anybody? A curtain separated the room—hello?—but no one answered from the bed on the other side.

He squinted at the big round clock on the wall in front of him. Maybe a little past eight? Night probably. On the whiteboard under the clock it said You are in room #280. Your Nurse is Karen. Something something. Gobble Gobble.

God, he was parched, his mouth sour and tasting of chemicals. He clenched and unclenched his good hand. Where was water? From the hall came the sound of clanking trays, maybe, and a vacuum. A little pitcher perched on the bedside table but when he reached toward it, the movement set off beeping and flashing green lights. He tried to push himself more upright when the nurse—Karen?—glided in, backlit by the hall lights.

"Ah, I see you're awake, Mr. Griffin." She pressed a couple buttons above his head and the beeping stopped. She reached up and gave the bag of fluid a little shake. "Come on wake up." She flicked the bag with her finger. "Sometimes it just needs a little talking too. There."

Karen peered down at him and touched his shoulder. "How are you?"

The finger. Marianne. His thirst.

"My finger... did I... I mean..."

"Oh. I hear it was ugly! But, it's still attached if that's what you mean. For now." She smiled. "The surgeon debrided it, and they're flooding you with a cocktail of antibiotics. They probably won't be in until morning to look at it and decide how to proceed."

He was ashamed. His finger was so infected, so ugly. "I tried to keep it clean. My wife, she cleaned it and re-bandaged it every day." He licked his dry lips, felt conscious that his breath was rank. "Is there water?"

"Oh, yes, we try to torture you and keep it just out of reach." She poured a cup and held it for him as he sipped from a straw.

Adam lay back against his pillows. "Thank you. Can you tell me what time it is and where my wife might be?"

"Aren't hospitals weird? So disorienting. It's just after eight. That would be p.m. And I sent your wife—Marianne?—down to the cafeteria to get something to eat before it closes. She looked pooped, poor thing." He liked the lightness in her voice, as if she'd just eaten something sweet.

Karen swung the bedside tray table closer and put the pitcher and a full cup of water on it. "She left you a couple things—looks like your phone and a picture."

"My dog, Banjo."

"Here's the call button. Call if you need anything. Okay?"

He didn't want her to leave. "Thank you."

He closed his eyes and held the call button in his good hand. He had the finger. For now. Thank you God thank you God thank you God. It was just a finger—not a leg, or an arm—but still. He should be grateful to be so lucky, but the surge of relief felt hunted by something dark and heavy. A cold rain began to chop against the big glass window. He was glad he had the heavy blankets on him, glad he was inside. Grateful.

When he woke, Marianne was sitting in the chair next to his bed. The glow of the low lights by the window illuminated her round face and hazel eyes and her tousle of hair—which she was doing something new to. "Warming it up with a little blonde," he thought he remembered her saying as she leaned over the tub rinsing her hair the other night.

"Babe." She leaned in with her tired face and kissed his cheek.

"Did you get to the cafeteria before it closed?" He pictured the cold dry turkey and congealed mashed potatoes left behind at home. Had she turned off the stove?

"I brought you some pumpkin pie," she pointed to a small Styrofoam container. "It's not bad."

Ambulance lights reeled outside the window behind her head.

"So, you did good taking care of my finger—it's still here. But you probably know that."

"And I did good by bringing you here."

"Yes." She was looking down at her clasped hands and didn't meet his eyes.

"I've been so mad at you lately," she whispered. "You knew your finger was bad, and you wouldn't tell me. I know you've been hiding the bills." She shook her head. "I'm sorry. Now's not the time."

Adam reached for her hand and closed his eyes. "I've let you down."

She dropped his hand. "Don't get like that—where now I need to comfort you and reassure you. No. That's not fair."

He was quiet, wanting her to keep talking but scared of what she might say.

"I know about the letters from the bank about the house. I'm working my ass off and trying to keep positive and get you back on your feet. But, I mean, my God." Marianne stood up and strode to the window.

"What Marianne?"

Tension defined every angle of her, shoulders, elbows, the long seams of her legs.

"The dog is dead. Lily doesn't write to you." She turned toward him. "You've made mistakes. But this is fucking it - " her arms spread wide, her face streamed with tears—"this is life. This is life. Why aren't we doing it together?"

The door swung open and two men in scrubs pushed in a bed with a large man on it and steered it behind the curtain. The man cursed and groaned.

Adam ached to know what Marianne would say next, to open the sheets and have her crawl in next to him. Slowly she gathered her coat from the chair and put it over her arm. It was like watching a movie where everyone in the audience is crying and it *is* moving—you'll tell people later how sad it was—but you just aren't feeling it and that makes you feel even worse because you know everyone else is.

"I love you, Marianne." It's true, he thought, I do.

Marianne raised her eyebrows. She had composed herself in that moment, pulled everything back inside. "I hope you get some sleep," she mouthed. Adam reached for her hand and she let him squeeze it before she slipped past the curtain and out the door.

Machines rolled in. People came and went, setting up and settling in this new roommate. Adam couldn't think with all the commotion. He wanted to think about what Marianne just said. What did it mean? He knew he should feel sad but should he feel scared? More scared?

He squeezed his eyes and wished he could put his fingers in his ears. *Be quiet.*

Cow-like bellows came from the bed behind the curtain. *Ohh. Ohh. Oh my God.* Adam looked up at his ghostly hand. Everything was stiff.

Oh my God it hurts so bad it hurts so bad.

Someone scurried in.

"I'm right here. What's going on now?" It wasn't Karen.

"Oh God you people have no idea how much this hip hurts. When can I get something for the pain?"

"Next pain meds are at four a.m. But I can get you more ice. How's that? And I'll let your nurse know." It wasn't a question. The answer came as more moans.

The nurse pulled aside a corner of the curtain on her way out.

"Sorry, Mr. Griffin. Hip replacement. I hope you can go back to sleep." She reminded him of a drill sergeant he had once—and the right person to deal with this roommate.

"I'll be fine. Thank you," he said.

She nodded and left, returning moments later to bring ice to his roomate. Sucking sounds came from the bed next door, the sucking of machines, moving fluids, the slurp of the patient sucking ice chips. What do you do to replace a hip? Lots of sawing, Adam imagined. Then, do they just throw away the old bone? His own hip ached thinking about it. He really needed sleep; suddenly he felt frantic for sleep. He pushed his call button.

Karen came in, with a blanket over one arm and a plastic basin in the other hand. "Yes, Mr. Griffin?" She flipped off the call button. He liked how she paused, like she had all the time in the world.

"I'm really having trouble sleeping in this position," he glanced up. "Do you know how long my hand has to hang like this?"

"It's important to keep it elevated to keep the swelling and pressure down. The surgeons won't be back around until about six a.m." She glanced at a clock on the wall. "It's just after midnight. Black Friday if you have any shopping to do." She smiled.

"Is it possible to take the hand down for a while? Just a bit so I can sleep?" Her smile encouraged him to push a little.

Karen put her things down on the foot of his bed. The pressure of the blanket against his feet reminded him of Banjo, who used to walk over to the bed and lay his head in just about that spot. Adam would wake up to the sound of Banjo's easy breath.

Hands on hip, Karen peered up at Adam's hand. "I'll tell you what. We'll prop it up on a stack of pillows for a while. It'll be a little more comfortable but still be elevated. Okay?" It wasn't a question.

"Thank you, Karen."

Caring Karen.

Karen located pillows from down the hall and loaded them on the side of his bed. As if she held a newborn chick, she lowered his hand down onto the pillows. "You're going to be all right," she said, sliding out of the room.

He tried to sleep to the song of the machines behind the curtain sucking and pumping and his neighbor groaning and thrashing. He should have told Marianne to call when she got home, just so he'd know she was safe. He couldn't even dial her like this. In the dark, full of poisons to chase other poisons, hopelessness and toxicity invaded him. He could feel the medicine in his blood whooshing through him. Was it blowing the infection to kingdom come or just spreading it through his body? He felt weighted down as if dirt and rocks covered him. Would he ever be free again? Light again? When had he last felt anything resembling joy? He opened his eyes and took the picture of Banjo from the bedside table and laid it on the pillow next to his hand. The dogs had always given him comfort, grounded him, you could say.

Where was Banjo? In the mayhem he'd forgotten—how could he have!?—what had become of Banjo's body? He had to put him with Humphrey. *He had to get Banjo.*

It was as though his brain could hold only the dark days; the finger, the empty dog bed, the potential disaster of the house, how he'd not been a good father to Lily, the sadness in Marianne. He tried to call in all the goodness—it was Thanksgiving after all—to drink it in and let everything else wash away. Marianne's face floated up above him, soft and hazy and melting into the ceiling. He'd never fixed the ceiling.

What had happened in that room just before Banjo died? Was he whispering in Banjo's ear? He'd meant to. Yes he'd been just starting that prayer his mother said to him sometimes when he was little. *Now I lay me down to sleep. I pray the lord my soul to keep. If I die before I wake, I pray the lord my soul to take.* He'd put those words in Banjo's ears so Banjo could float away or dissolve or transform or go to God knowing he was not alone.

Now I lay me down to sleep I pray the lord my soul to keep and if I die before I wake I pray the lord my soul to take. Nowilaymedowntosleepipraythelordmy-soultokeepandifidiebeforeiwakeipraythelordmysoultotakenow

"Will you Goddamn be quiet? I can't sleep over here!"

You can hear me?

"Are you talking to me?" he called above the noises in the room. Who was this guy to bellow about being quiet anyway?

"Who the hell else would I be talking to? What're you here for anyway?"

What am I here for anyway?

"I don't know."

"Well you're worse off than I am. Least I know I got my Goddamn hip replaced."

"My dog bit me." His finger twitched and touched Banjo's picture.

"Turned on ya, did he?"

Did he turn on me?

A band of light shone in from the hall. Behind the curtain Karen said, "Four a.m. You can have your pain meds now."

"No," Adam whispered even though his roommate couldn't hear him and wasn't listening any more. He pictured Marianne, her cool hands smoothing his forehead. He pictured Lily watching him from her bedroom window. He pictured something warm and tiny and needy filling the empty dog bed. He saw Karen's kind face, like the waxing moon, passing by the foot of his bed. *"You're going to be all right."*

He pictured Banjo's great big maw opening up and coming down hard.

No he didn't turn on me.

Adam saw his own hand levitating, rising, pulling him up with it.

Phantom Pain

The pink terry cloth tie from her bathrobe has fallen from the hook and is lying on the floor. Katherine picks it up. She's tired this morning, can't stay afloat, all the adrenaline that pumped through her after Eddie's accident and the first couple weeks home, just gone. She won't go for her early morning swim in the pond, not with the rain. She's got to find ways to keep up her energy and her spirit, or they will both keep sinking. If he took the pain pills she left out for him with a glass of water, Eddie should still be sleeping on the foldout couch in the den downstairs. Or perhaps he is awake and waiting for her to come in with coffee. He is careful, it seems, not to call her, knowing as he does after twenty-four years together that a small slice of morning solitude is the base on which she builds her day. Either way, he certainly can't walk in on her.

Still holding the bathrobe tie, Katherine pulls her right foot up behind her, like before a run when she's stretching. It's hard to balance. This isn't quite right, Eddie's amputation is mid-thigh, but it gives her a feeling. She sinks to the cool tile floor, her foot still bent behind her. She shimmies the tie under her ankle and ties her ankle to her thigh as tight as she can, so tight she worries about cutting off the blood supply. Somehow it feels urgent to get it right and her palms burn as she pulls the terry cloth and knots it. It is harder to get off the floor than she thought, as if more than part of her leg is missing. Looking for handholds and a way to pull herself up, she notices the dusty baseboards and strands of hair in the corner. She'll have to get in here later, on her hands and knees and scrub.

She pulls herself to standing and looks in the mirror. She's lost all perspective lately. Is she beautiful or plain? From certain angles and in certain light, her younger self appears, sharp and capable, radiating energy. And beautiful; she can say that now, can't she, now that she isn't? Eddie always said she was. But he didn't find much fault with her, not until the accident when there are so many things she can't seem to do right—the bandage is too tight, he can't get comfortable, and she is no help with the pillows. It always annoyed her, how he never seemed bothered by her the way she could be bothered by him. By little things, like putting the cereal box back in the cupboard when it was empty. By the bigger things, like when he held things inside for so long. How come he didn't have criticisms of her? *He thinks you're perfect*, her mother would say, but that couldn't be. It made her feel like he didn't really see her anymore. Like he loved her due to habit. She turns and catches sight of the older woman that is emerging, that she will eventually become. It isn't just physical, the loosening of the flesh at her neck or the downward slope of everything, but there is vagueness to her energy, the unattractive look of the lost.

Her foot is beginning to tingle. She hops into the bedroom. If she had Eddie's crutches, she could practice with those and try to find ways to encourage Eddie, who is having difficulty with them. He says he fears the second where his foot must lift up and swing forward, when all he has to rely on is these two little rubber discs, no bigger than sand dollars to hold all of his weight. As an architect, he'd tell people, a strong foundation is essential for a building to soar.

She takes a breather at his bureau, resting her palm on it to steady herself. In the center of the bureau, Megan, age 19, smiles in rapture from the 14,000 foot summit of Longs Peak, which she climbed in July, during a break from her summer ranger job in the Rockies. Katherine considers the photo of Megan, the hood of her red windbreaker around her face, the escaped hair whirling, her leg with the gash on the shin from climbing through something called the Key Hole, which, Megan reported, had winds at 62 mph on that day. She flew home after the accident, when Eddie was still in the hospital, bringing into that dark time a splash of bright color. She runs her fingertip around Megan's face then hops on, from one side of the room to the other side of the room and round again, until the muscles in her shoulders ache and her "good" leg has a shooting pain right up to her hip socket.

Katherine stands outside the door and listens for Eddie on her way to the kitchen, but all is quiet. He so badly needs a good night sleep. This is the first morning in a long while that she has to turn on the light to make the coffee. The tin has just enough coffee for a small pot. She shakes the cream carton; barely a drop. The refrigerator, recently full, due to the kindness of friends and neighbors, is empty enough for her to see the box of baking soda, usually obscured. She hasn't been to the grocery store in three weeks. Maybe the freezer is harboring something she can thaw for dinner. The thought of seeing people, of being asked, 'How is he? How are *you* doing?' makes her feel frantic. She waits for the coffee to perk and realizes she is more afraid of the day people stop asking, as if it is all over. Today, standing at her counter, looking out at the rain, she can't conjure up how they will get back to normal.

Two cups of coffee in hand, she bumps open the door of the den with a shoulder. The room has a stale airless smell.

"Oh, God, Eddie, you should have called me." He's fallen out of bed. She sets down the coffee and pushes open the curtains. Pearly gray light spills in. She kneels down beside him, wanting to help, even though Dr. Phillips said she shouldn't, not anymore.

"I thought you were going to come through the ceiling." He raises his eyebrows at her but she won't say anything about her little experiment. Eddie's good leg is stretched out in front of him and his stump, in the stump binder to reduce swelling, is hidden in his flannel pajamas.

"I bet you can get yourself back up there." She slowly stands and reaches again for her coffee. It is like Eddie's lost all muscle memory, control, will. Of course, he needs to heal and relearn how his body works. But slumped against the bed, palms up, he looks so passive, and that is a state of mind, right?

"Have a sip," she holds the coffee out to him, but he shakes her off. Inside, she's feeling chaos, like she did when Megan was small and stubborn, refusing to do what Katherine wanted her to do. The right tactic could be anything from cajoling to threatening, but she never seemed to know.

Eddie's brown hair is threaded with gray and needs a wash. Robert, the visiting nurse ,will be here this morning, and he will help him shower. On the table is the bottle of the narcotic du jour, cap off, zero refills left. There's a wet spot on his blue Rocky Mountain High t-shirt Megan gave him, like he drank his water lying down. He won't look up at her.

She sits cross-legged next to him.

"Well, how was your night?"

"Pretty rotten." But he takes the coffee.

She misses the first days home. They were tender toward each other, as, in shock, they learned new roles. He needed so much from her, help in the bathroom, help getting dressed, to be held in the night when the phantom leg pain nearly drove him crazy. In the light of day, he was grateful, stoic, and careful with her. And, for Katherine, finding a routine, however jarring, was a great relief after the confusion of the accident. She felt purposeful, laser sharp, everything extraneous washed away. They got in the habit of watching *Who Wants to Be a Millionaire* every day at 1 p.m., answering the questions out loud. It was almost like a vacation. Almost. It reminded her when they brought Megan home from the hospital, a little seven-pound terror. She and Eddie were equally lost, but a team.

A light rain thrums against the side of the house. The windows are steamed, and she has a desire to draw in the steam with her finger. SOS.

"I skipped my morning swim today. I might not be able to force myself into the pond again until next June." She reaches out her fingers and puts them on his arm. He's getting slack, soft, even the muscles in his forearm which have never failed to give her a little surge of lust. His skin is dry. She pulls her fingers back.

"All this rain. Is the dam holding?" Eddie flicks his eyes up to hers, and she's gratified at his attempt to engage in conversation.

"Seems to be. I guess I wouldn't know until the whole thing just burst."

"You need to look for cracks, leaks, chinks, spillage—"

"Okay. Okay. I'll go down later and look."

It is quiet for a long time.

"You know, Dr. Phillips suggested—"

"—that I do things for myself, that I buck up and learn how to ski on one leg or, for God sakes, be grateful that I'm not a quadriplegic or dead even."

She can't even look at him. How did they get here? How will they get out of here? They were fine, yes readjusting to life without Megan around, yes she was going through a mini-mid-life crisis, but they were fine.

The books lining the walls over his head look messy; why hasn't she noticed this before? That would be a project, organizing the books by topic or alphabetically or maybe by date of publication. Or just pack some of her favorites up and send them to Megan at college. She feels dizzy. She wants to dig deep inside herself and absorb his anger, put herself in his place, but she also wants to start throwing things at him.

"Okay, Eddie." She stands up and starts to walk when he grabs her ankle.

"You want to leave, don't you?"

"I'm not doing any good at the moment. Obviously. Let go." He's still strong.

"I mean leave. Leave." His voice like a fist in her solar plexus.

Leaving. Here they are back at the conversation they were engaged in the morning of his accident. What if he hadn't been angry at her? Would he have been more careful and calm? Would he have moved more slowly and listened more attentively to the creaks and groans and whirrs of the blade as it became wedged? What are accidents anyway? Lapse in attention, carelessness, unpreventable flukes, fate, God's will, freaks of nature, someone else's fault? Maybe all of the above.

"No, Eddie." She shakes her head at him, disbelieving that he is stuck on this point. "It was an intellectual question. Let it go. And please let go of my ankle. Robert's coming soon. And after that, if the sun comes out, I'll take you down to the pond."

Sun. They were eating breakfast at the kitchen table, the sun spilling in, everything bright and shimmering with August heat. She'd been reading an article about how much longer people are living these days, and how, therefore, marriages can last many decades. After a point, let's say child rearing, is monogamy natural, useful, realistic, the article posed the question. She'd read this to Eddie, *With 52% of marriages ending in divorce, with the statistics for infidelity unreliable but shockingly high, are humans attempting to achieve something which goes against their animal nature? Is it time to redefine cultural expectations around the usefulness of monogamy?*

"You should leave me. Jeez, will you look at me, Katherine?" He loosens his grip on her ankle, but she can still feel the warmth of his palm. She can barely look at him because Eddie, helpless, terrifies her.

"Here, Eddie, let me help you up."

"We were in the middle of a conversation when I sawed my goddamn leg off."

"Forget it. It was stupid. Everything I said, just forget it." She squats down and scoots her arms under his to help him on the couch.

What she'd said: *Aren't you ever curious? Don't you ever wonder what it would be like to be with someone else?* He said, Well sure, in a vague, male-fantasy way. He'd been eating peanut butter on a bagel, and he was making that dry clicking sound with his tongue that drove her crazy. And she pushed. They met freshman year in college. She'd barely ever been with anyone else in her life, and it seemed important to at least discuss it. He kept giving her pat, funny answers until she got mad. Then the conversation took on some warped, spiraling energy, which ended with Eddie pushing back his chair. "Just what is your problem this morning?" And he abandoned her with the breakfast dishes and a raw restless feeling.

The doorbell rings. Robert, a relief. Walking through the mud-room to let in Robert, it jars her—still—to see the wheelchair. Last week, she finally cleared space, not just the little path she'd made by scooting over Eddie's sneakers and work boots, a pair of rain boots and her gardening clogs. No she went in there with two boxes and a garbage bag. She threw out a rotting pair of her sneakers, but put all of Eddie's footwear in a box to go into the basement where they would be when he needed them. She couldn't bear to throw out the right shoes. The sled, a hand saw, and a footstool, all were returned to their rightful place—basement, shed, closet. And old mouse trap went into the trash. Now there is room to maneuver the wheelchair. It is a relief to have the clutter gone.

She hears the shower running and sits down at the table to pay bills, glad that someone else is taking care of Eddie. She writes the checks carefully, balancing the checkbook, filing away the bills. Robert and Eddie are talking.

"What do you remember?" Robert's voice is low and soothing. Eddie likes him because his movements are so calm and confident; she knows this because he told her so the other day as she banged the wheelchair through a doorway.

"Things moved so fast. The tree was rotten up top, I guess. It's cliché, but it happened in a split second."

She puts her pen down. She can't imagine that moment of terror and has been afraid to ask.

"Did you think you were going to die?" Bless Robert.

"It's true what they say, your life passing in front of you. Ouch." They must be doing his exercises. "It was like chaos, but everything was there."

Katherine pictures standing in a windstorm in the fall, leaves of every bright color imaginable swirling around her, each leaf a moment, a word, a face, a passion, a mistake, a sadness, a joy.

"I was so fucking afraid. I thought—I don't know if you can really call it thought, maybe I was consumed by the thought– but what if I never saw Megan and Katherine again."

Does he not blame her? She wants to rush in, but she can't move.

Of course he doesn't blame her for the accident. But there is so much anger and sadness free-floating around the house now, massive and heavy and amorphous.

The sun angles through a hole in the cloud and spills onto the table where she sits. This September day won't get any nicer, or warmer, than it is right now. The water still holds some summer warmth. A swim is doable, and she needs to do it, needs to add things back into her days. Changing into her suit, she hears Robert call up that he'll be back on Wednesday. She wants to run down and ask him how he thinks Eddie's doing, offer him coffee, see if she can keep him here a little bit longer. But he leaves before she can get decent.

Downstairs Eddie is clean, shaven, in fresh clothes sitting in the wheelchair at the table having some toast.

"You look nice. What do you have on the stove?"

"Hard boiling some eggs. Part of my therapy, Robert says, taking care of myself."

He hasn't turned on the stove fan and steam rises and coats the clock.

"Excellent." She flips the switch for the fan. Only 9:30. The day feels very old already. "After you eat, let's go down to the pond." If she makes her voice bright, perhaps they will follow, even though the feeling of sinking that she woke with lingers. But sinking is easy, and this feels hard, like climbing.

She runs the eggs under cold water for a second and then scoops out the insides into a bowl for Eddie. While he eats, she sits opposite him with a pad of paper trying to make a grocery list. At some point, she'll have to go. She cannot imagine anything ever tasting flavorful again.

"I need prune juice," Eddie says finally.

Prune juice. How she'd like to think of something funny to say, but all the humorous lines about prunes seem depressing. *Prune juice.* She writes it down.

She gives Eddie her towel, slips on her flip flops and maneuvers the wheel chair through the door and down the ramp that she had installed while he was in the hospital. Besides doctors' appointments, this will be their first outing. God give her strength to push him through the grass down to the pond and then back up. Going down is okay, the path firm under her feet, the wheels gripping. It is so unbelievable that he can't just get up and walk. Maybe someday soon once he gets the prosthetic. But, even so, to see him run was a beautiful thing, and she won't, he won't, not like that ever again. She parks him on the grass by the sand. They're losing the sun to gray, scudding clouds.

Katherine feels his eyes on her as she peels off her sweats. It doesn't feel like it used to, when she knew his looks were full of admiration. She feels guilty for having two strong legs, taking her into the water in long strides.

The water is cold and heavy like wet leaves after a rain, dense against her skin. Her scalp aches and her bones feel stiff, but after a while she reaches a rhythm and begins to come to life, with the heat in her lungs and the blood rushing to her muscles. She pulls the water with her hands, flat like fish, and kicks so she can feel the muscles in the front of her thighs. She can just make out the little motes that hang suspended by strands of sun. She'll take this as a message from God, shine a little light in the dark and see all the life that is there. She begins to dive down in little, tiny dolphin dives that take her into darker and colder pockets of the pond. It strikes her like a wave, that all she wanted was to know that Eddie would choose her again. That he sees her—beautiful, ugly, the whole package—but that he loves her because he knows her and would choose to be with her again. She cries underwater, like a humpback whale, until she is too cold to go on.

When she gets out, Eddie hands her the towel. She sits in the sand and leans against his knee. Eddie puts his hand on her head and strokes her hair. Will he lean forward and kiss her neck or touch her breast? How they took for granted how easy everything was. She's terrified he won't ever touch her that way again, just as terrified imagining that first encounter.

When she shivers Eddie drapes her sweatshirt over her shoulders. He's been keeping it warm. She slips it on and shakes her wet hair loose from the neck.

"I thought, my God, what if you got a cramp and started drown-ing, I couldn't do anything," Eddie says softly. "You shouldn't swim by yourself. Not anymore. Freak accidents happen." He makes a little noise like the beginning of a laugh. She doesn't want to turn, in case he's weeping. She knows she will not be able to hold it together, not on this gray day when the grass smells like autumn and the leaves on the birch tree are turning pale yellow and everything is completely different. She feels his knee on her back and rocks gently into it.

"Let's go back up Eddie." She wants to feel hot water cascading down her shoulders. "While I take a shower you can do more O.T. and make us some hot chocolate." When will they stop circling?

"I'll race you," Eddie says putting his hands on the push-rims. Katherine knows what an effort he is making for her. He can't get himself unstuck from where his front tires have wedged into the soft ground. She watches him strain and use his foot to push the chair to a place where he can get traction. Her fingers are numb with cold. She waits while they both pretend this is something he can do.

It begins to rain again. She goes around behind him without saying anything and tugs the chair. Eddie doesn't resist as she pushes him up the hill to the house. Her flip-flops slip and so she leaves them by the path, digging in with her toes.

The Voice at the End of the Line

Somewhere a phone is ringing. It is ringing and ringing, and she's trying to get to there, moving through leafy foliage and then parting curtains of tiny bright beads, and it rings‑

Oh God, who's calling in the middle of the night? Valerie knocks over a glass as she finds the phone on top of a stack of magazines she's been meaning to read.

"Yes?" Her mouth is sticky and there is a red‑wine headache puls‑ing under her scalp.

"Mom?" Delia's voice can sound so accusing.

"What's wrong?"

"Where have you been?"

Valerie holds the phone away from her ear. She still has on her earrings and the necklace with the diamond "V" that Jeb gave her before he left them for good. She can hear blood in her ears, whooshing.

"Delia, I'm here. It's—" she gets up on an elbow and looks over the sleeping shape of—oh Christ—is Frank still here? "It's 2:04 a.m."

The annual meeting of the entire North American sales force has brought Frank, from Lincoln, Nebraska to town. He rolls over, throws an arm around her like she is as familiar as his wife, whom they never discussed after that first meeting five years ago.

"I've called your cell phone all night and then paged you, too." Delia's voice is rising.

"What's up?" Frank says, eyes barely open, rolling the barrel of his body toward Valerie, who puts a finger to his lips to shush him.

"Mom, who's there?" Delia, *the girl who could hear through walls.* The girl who knew before Valerie did that Jeb had secrets to keep.

"Is this why you called, hon?" Gently, she puts the phone on her other ear and curls onto her side away from Frank, whose odors are unfamiliar and now unwelcome. They gravitate toward each other every year at these annual meetings. Valerie wonders how she would explain it to Delia if she had that notion. It's not lust. It's loneliness. She wishes he would leave and snugs the sheet more firmly around herself.

"No. I just. It's been. Well, a bad night, let's just say." Delia's voice sounds teensy, squeezed, as if it really is coming in through wires stretched between the two of them, all these 200 miles.

"What happened?" Valerie sits up, the sheet around her, aware of the sloshing in her head, the stickiness between her legs. She wants an aspirin, a shower, Frank to leave; she has a sudden lurch of *wanting* that just scoops her out, and she has to lean her elbows on her knees and get steady.

"What's up?" Frank says in a whisper so loud it echoes and when his damp hand touches the small of her back through the sheet, she stands up.

"Mother? Who is that?" Poor Delia, her fierce little bodyguard of a child, unable to give it up even now in college, always putting herself in front of Valerie, hands on her hips, challenging the men whom she let wander into their lives.

"It's a friend, okay?" She says it gently, as in don't worry, baby, he won't hurt me. Us. You. She moves away from the bed as far as the cord will go and kicks her feet through the pile of clothes on the floor, wondering where the cordless phone is. A wedge of street light comes in when she parts the curtains to run her fingers on the windowsill. She knocks over a bottle of nail polish and feels soft dust on her fingertips. Christ, where is that phone?

"Can you just hang on a sec, baby, I want to find the cordless." She sets the receiver back down on her bedside table and uprights the tipped glass. The dull orange light coming in from outside is enough for her to gather up Frank's pants, jingling with coins and heavy with the belt and his shirt, name tag—*Frank O'Brien, Northwest Quadrant Sales Rep* - pinned on the breast pocket. His underwear must be somewhere at the bottom of the bed.

"Frank. Time to go." The clothes land on the bed in a soft thump. He pulls his clothes in toward him, but his eyes are still closed. "Hold on, Del," she calls into the phone and goes into the bathroom. She wets a wash cloth and dabs it with soap and washes between her legs. She rinses her mouth with water and puts on the flannel pajamas with the pink roses, softened by years of washing and wearing, hanging on the hook behind the door. She's kept the light off, afraid of seeing the worn out lipstick, the mussed hair, the wrinkles around her eyes.

"Go already, Frank," she hisses at him when it is clear he has burrowed back into the warmth of the bed.

In the living room, two martini glasses sit on the coffee table, hers with the olive still in it. She spies the phone next to her black sling backs on the floor. "I'm back," she tells Delia, while going to hang up the other extension. She holds the phone between her shoulder and ear, shutting the door and Frank and his smells—faded cologne, the clingy scent of the cigar he chewed on but didn't light, the smell of his sweat—and curls up on the living room couch in the dim light coming from the street through the gauzy curtains.

"Okay, babe. I'm here." She pulls the orange and yellow afghan Aunt Natalie knit her one Christmas over her knees. Her head thrums, she should have popped some ibuprofen.

"Where are you?" Delia, her strong, fierce little girl sounds fragile, maybe teary.

Maybe something is wrong. Maybe she's not just checking up on her. She didn't even think of that; self-centered, just like Jeb accused her all those years ago.

"I'm sitting on the couch in the living room. It has new pillows; you'll see them at Thanksgiving," she says gently. "Are you okay? What is it, babe?"

"Talk to me some more, Mom." Delia makes snuffling noises into a tissue.

Valerie feels a cool tingle of air from the window brushing her neck and realizes that she's afraid.

"Well, um, let's see—" she fumbles, wonders what Delia wants. What she needs to hear. "Oh, I think Furball has a girlfriend." Furball is their thirteen-year old cat who slinks toward her now. "He wants to go out all the time, and he doesn't come back till all hours, but he never looks ragged or like he's been in a fight. I think it might be this little orange cat I see down the street, where the Jacksons used to live?" Perhaps she's rambling; perhaps this isn't what Delia needs to hear. But when she pauses it is very quiet.

"I've been busting my you-know-whatski for this convention. We have five hundred sales reps here, and I tell you, some of them totally need their hand held. I mean, I make up these packets with maps, agendas, name tags, emergency phone numbers, and lists of places to eat, coupons to restaurants, taxi services, movie theaters. They ask me questions all day long. God, you would think that some of these people never left—"

"Shut up, Mom."

"Okay." Valerie stops weaving her fingers through the afghan, stops breathing.

"You know what happened to me tonight?" Delia's voice is accusing. "I got drunk and went back to some stupid frat house with some good-looking shithead."

Valerie's mouth feels greasy like she might be sick. "Did he hurt you? Are you okay?" She feels small and uncertain.

"*Did he hurt you? Are you okay?*" Delia mimics her.

Valerie looks at her hands. They are trembling. Furball jumps up on the couch.

"Sometimes we do stupid things. Things happen. I don't want you beating yourself up on top of everything else."

"*Things happen?* We don't somehow create the environment where they can happen? We don't internalize shit so that we let them happen?"

"Well, that too. I know I—"

"Well, we all know *you.* You could have beat yourself up just a little bit over it, now and then. The freak shows you brought home. My God, Mother."

Valerie is assaulted by a memory of Brick, a boyfriend she had for a time. He'd told her once, lying in bed, rolling a beaded necklace that Delia made her between his thumb and forefinger, "If I were you, I'd keep a really tight leash on D." She could feel his fingers pressing the beads against her collar bones. "What's that supposed to mean?" She looked at his white teeth and the scar by his lip from a hockey puck, praying for something fatherly and wise to come out of his mouth. "She's turning out to be quite a beauty and—don't take this wrong—a tease." She remembers—feels again now—revulsion lurching inside her. How fucking dare he think that about her beautiful thirteen-year old daughter? She didn't say anything, just got up and showered, made him bacon and eggs and, while he ate, jammed all his things in a trash bag and threw it out the back door.

"I'm sorry." Valerie doesn't know what else to say. The bathroom door closes, and she hears the shower.

"God, what were you thinking?" Delia says.

"I don't know." Valerie's throat is closing around her voice, shrinking it.

"That's my point, Mom, you didn't know." Delia is loud now. Furball kneads the blanket.

"Yes. Yes, you're right." She pets Furball with her shaking hands, remembering Lionel who broke a whiskey bottle—smash—against the head of her bed and then looked at his hand with the blood dripping down it and told her, "it's all your fault."

"But, Delia, look at you. You are so beautiful and smart and in college—"

"Are you listening?" Delia speaks as if to a foreigner. "Me. Drunk. Tonight. Went home with I don't even know who. And you know how that makes me feel? Like you. Like you at your worst. Like you at your most pathetic." Delia's voice is sharpening even as Valerie's image of her is dissolving, watery. She has a bursting feeling in her chest as Delia begins to cry.

Valerie holds the phone very close to her ear and imagines Delia's head on her shoulder. She can't remember Delia crying, though that cannot be true. How can a child not cry? How can a mother not remember?

She imagines Delia's silky brown hair falling over her face, and she wishes she could touch it and hold her. Inside, she feels like she is crumpling, as if Del's tears were her own. When was the last time *she* cried? How do feelings of pain or sadness inspire the body to make tears? And to what end?

She remembers opening the back door on a fall day, oh God was it sharp and bright and painfully beautiful. She had a hangover—the thick headache and bitter stomach—and her coffee mug sloshed in her shaky hand as she pushed open the screen. Delia was rounded into a little ball, her forehead on her knees, the pea green Fair Isle sweater she insisted on wearing every day, not long enough to reach her knobby wrists. She must have been about ten. Valerie remembers sitting down next to her. The back steps needed fresh paint, and she picked at a loose chip with her finger nail. The grass needed mowing, and it was growing in places, like the walkway and the flowerbeds, where it shouldn't. She'd put her arm around her daughter and pulled her in under her arm.

Valerie, with the phone on her shoulder and Delia's little sobs in her ear, cannot remember why Delia was crying that day, cannot remember how that little scene resolved itself. And why that moment, among all others, pops into her head right now.

"Delia." She says it softly over and over.

"Yeah?"

"Do you remember the pea green sweater you wore every day for a year?"

"I can't believe you remember it." Delia makes a honking noise.

"What does that mean?" She says, she hopes, tenderly.

"You weren't exactly mother-of-the-year then."

Valerie is struck—as if this is a new or original thought—by the distance, real or imagined, between two people.

Images rush at her, how Delia used to chew her pencils when she was thinking, how she used to fill her bowl with Rice Krispies and milk right to the very rim and not spill a drop, how she would leap from the area rug to her bed even into her teens, claiming she was afraid of what might be under the bed, those beaded necklaces she turned out by the dozens one icy winter, cross-legged at the coffee table with her bowl of beads while the radio played.

Valerie pushes Furball off her lap and untangles herself from the afghan. She meets Frank in the hall, covers the phone with one hand and tells him goodbye, and keeps moving. In her jewelry box, in the underneath part, she finds the tangle of beads.

"Hey, Del," she holds them in one hand like precious gems, holds the phone with the other hand, "Hold on a sec." She spills the necklaces out onto her bureau and sorts through until she has three untangled, and then she puts them around her neck. Teeny tiny beads like baby teeth, she thinks as she unhooks the sparkling V which she's quite sure is not made of real diamonds.

"Ok," she says, "I'm here."

Between the Dream and Here

Martha dreamt that she was wearing her shawl made of one thousand Hail Marys. Except in the dream, Martha was young, climbing an apple tree in her parents' orchard with her long hair waving down her back like sunlit water. The shawl, a dusky mauve color, was tied around her waist like she was a gypsy girl. She looked down at her best friend Kate, standing under the tree with her arms around herself. Martha had called Kate chicken and climbed higher and higher until there was just sky in her hands.

Martha lies like a bag of bones in her Lay-Z-Boy recliner. When she awakes, she whispers, "Water, Candace, bring me water." She's so thirsty it's as if she really climbed that tree on a hot summer day. She can hear Candace humming in the kitchen and water running in the sink. She pulls the mauve prayer shawl, a gift from the women's fellowship group at the church, tight around her bony shoulders.

"Good morning, dear! Good morning, Mrs. Waterman!" Candace comes in the living room with a dish towel over her shoulder and a glass of water in her hand.

Martha takes the glass from Candace's chubby paw with its purple fingernails. She looks around and feels somehow stuck between the dream and here, this room. The sun in the dream felt strong and Kate's face was *there*, at the end of her outstretched hand. Things look familiar - the beige phone on the side table, the blue afghan in her lap, the "little people" stuck to the table with glue because they kept falling off and Mary and Jesus should not be on the green carpet. None of this is foreign, yet she can't place herself in it. And these hands—her hands sitting in her lap, lumpy bones under insubstantial skin, the blue veins like bruises and her wedding bands, platinum channel set with diamonds and sapphire, loose between her knuckles where they used to fit snug on her smooth skin. Not hers. Can't be.

Martha sips her water and sets the glass on the table. She closes her eyes again and tries to return to the warm vagueness of her nap. Distantly, the phone rings.

Candace pokes her head—is she a bit blonder today?—around the door frame separating the kitchen from the living room,

"It's Lauren on the phone—you wanna talk to her?"

Martha pictures Lauren pushing the intercom button on her office phone with a red fingernail and instructing her secretary to dial up Martha. In Martha's mind's eye, Lauren is tapping her leather boots and spiraling a pencil between her fingers. Martha turns away from Candace, who is shaking the phone at her. No, she shakes her head, No.

No, she won't talk to Lauren, at least not now. Her elbow hurts from when she fell out of bed on it a week ago. Whenever her granddaughter calls, the family has had a meeting and has some *issues* they'd like to discuss with Martha, about her health, about her living situation, because "We care about you, Granny."

Lauren has been chosen as the family spokesperson. She lives the closest to Martha, but Martha believes that Lauren would have been the chosen one no matter where she lived. Martha's only son, Raymond, is a good man, but Martha knows he is not strong enough to face her creeping decrepitude. Lauren, well,... sometimes Martha believes that the child who would curl up in her lap and play with Martha's earrings and the gold bangle she always wore was kidnapped by aliens and replaced with the Harvard lawyer who could stare down a bear.

Candace brings her oatmeal drizzled with maple syrup sitting in a pool of milk. Just the way she likes it.

"We're going to weigh you after breakfast, Mrs. Waterman, the doctor says so. Eat this up. I should weigh myself, don't you think?! But I'm going the other way." She pats her poochy tummy and laughs. "And then we are going to call your granddaughter back, she says it is *very* important."

Martha holds the warm oatmeal in her lap. Her arm feels shaky and a little milk dribbles off the spoon on to her pink pajama top. Candace, kneeling by her chair, carefully dabs it off, "What, you need a bib now?" Martha likes her sparkling earrings.

Martha rolls her eyes.

"What do you want to do today, Mrs. Waterman?"

The only scheduled activities Martha has anymore are the doctor and the beauty parlor, but not today. She knows if she sat in her chair all day and listened to music or a book on tape that would be enough, but Candace loves a bit of fun and Martha tries to please.

"My toes. Why don't you do my toes today? I like your purple finger nails. " The warm oatmeal slides down easily; she's hungry.

"I was hoping you'd say that! I just happen to have some nail polish in the back of my car." Candace stands and yanks open the curtains of the picture window.

This news does not surprise Martha. Though she's never ridden in the back of Candace's battered, tan Ford Escort, anything and everything the two of them have ever needed in the five months since Candace has been looking after Martha seems to be in the back of that car: a curling iron, a bag of salt and vinegar potato chips, size eight circular knitting needles, Elmer's glue. Sometimes, Martha feels like Mary Poppins has come to stay.

Martha lifts the bowl off her lap and hands it to Candace. A flickering of sun and shadow in the middle of the room catches her eye and Candace says, "Hey! Look at that fat grouse in the tree!"

Martha's neck hurts to turn it, as if it is hardening a little each day, all those little bones that connect the top of her spine to her head. A fat grouse, indeed two, are weighing down the branches of the crab apple tree as they feast on the berries. It was their sudden arrival in the tree, with the sun behind them that caused shadows to fly around the room. Martha turns her head back and closes her eyes for a minute.

"Let's start with a bath and getting some clothes on you, Mrs. Waterman."

Candace helps her into the wheel chair, and they roll into the bathroom. The first time Candace wedged her hands under Martha's knees and around her waist to ease her into her shower chair, Martha felt humiliated. Now she is long past worrying what Candace thinks about her naked, wasted body. Letting things go, one after the other.

Candace hangs Martha's shawl and pink pajamas on the hook on the back of the bathroom door. She holds her own hand under the spray and then declares, "It's ready for you now, princess." As the hot water melts her shoulders, Candace tells her a story about an "old, fat ham" she used to care for. He was so heavy that, "His peepee was as tiny as a new born baby's. But, you get him in the shower and it grew like a darn stalk of corn, with me the sun. Yee God. Can you picture it? So, you know what I did?! I turned that water on cold." She throws her head back and laughs at the thought. Martha, her eyes closed to the steam, giggles with her—when was the last time she laughed?— and hangs onto the bars. Candace hums, and the mirror fogs up, and Martha suddenly worries what would happen if Candace went away or if she had to leave her home? Martha starts to cry, hot silent tears.

"Okay, now, Mrs. Waterman," Candace says as she pries Martha's fingers from the metal hand rails. "Wow, you're as strong as a baby! You know how they grip your finger until the blood stops? I've got you now."

Candace helps Martha into soft camel colored pants and a light blue cashmere sweater with tiny buttons. She wants to look nice every day, no matter that she will put on slippers and wrap herself in a shawl because she is always cold now. Sometimes when Lauren drops by she'll say with surprise, "Granny, don't you look lovely! If I were you though, I'd stay in my jammies all day; that would be so much more comfortable."

The day she doesn't get out of her pajamas is the day she has given up, has decided to join Richard in heaven or wherever he went off to in 1989. Martha has very little to be vain about anymore, but she can still present herself through her attire. She used to be vain about her hair, long and shiny as a Breck girl's hair. And she was vain about her slim ankles and artistic looking hands. She knew her eyes could speak worlds, or so people said. But now, when she receives compliments they usually pertain to bodily functions—oh, aren't you a wonder to still be able to hear so well! Are those your real teeth; now isn't that fantastic.

Martha settles back in her chair to watch the Premium Shoppers Network with the adorable morning host Lisa. Her credit card is tucked under the phone. Martha loves watching PSN. The hostesses are spunky and full of enthusiasm, and first she watched just for the company. But one day, a deal on a forty-four piece, dishwasher safe set of plastic storage containers had her dialing in to order. Martha gave the plastic-ware to her next door neighbor, a tired looking mother with three young children who nonetheless sometimes shoveled Martha's walk or brought in her mail.

Maybe she'll find something today for Candace, like a pretty shawl or a piece of luggage with wheels. Something girly, luxurious, or something she can really use.

It had been Lauren who had found Candace for her, one of three women presented to Martha for her ultimate approval. Lauren had experience hiring secretaries, law clerks, cleaning help and nannies, so, after the family gathered round Martha on a Monday evening to implore her to get help, Lauren volunteered to take charge.

"We can't sleep at night worrying about you," Lauren spoke and everyone nodded, "and I'm going to find you someone with top references and don't worry about the cost." Everyone nodded again. Lauren had that effect on people.

Candace had knocked at the front door while turning the knob and letting herself in.

"Hello! It's Candace here for the interview!"

Lauren had greeted her and then led her to the kitchen and the boot tray and coat rack near the back door saying, "We're not quite ready for you yet, Candace. Have a seat in the kitchen." Lauren could put you in your place.

"A little pushy?" Lauren had mouthed to Martha when she came back into the living room. Martha had heard Candace humming and walking softly about the kitchen; she'd liked her immediately.

Out of the corner of her eye, Martha sees the grouse have left the crab apples to the little chickadees. How the chickadees keep warm on a winter day is a miracle. Martha is glad for the puddle of sun in her lap, though she is slightly chilled and her arm throbs.

Candace brings a waft of cold air in with her as she places the mail that she has just fetched from the mailbox on her table.

"I got it!" Candace dangles a little cosmetic bag in front of her.

"Good. I hope you have pink in there; red or purple toenails would be unseemly on someone of my age," Martha says. She allows Candace to take off her slippers and then she closes her eyes while Candace first smoothes cream that smells like the ocean on her feet, and then puts cotton balls between her toes and paints her toenails a terrific pink. Candace's hands are always warm. Heavenly.

"You know, you can call Lauren while your toes dry, Mrs. Waterman." Candace slips the nail polish back into her bag.

"She's really tightening the screws on me to move into a nursing home." Martha squints down at her sinfully pink toenails.

"She loves you so much, you know. You're lucky. Well, that's one way to look at it."

Martha knows she is lucky to have family that cares, but it also feels as if Raymond and Alicia and Lauren are conspiring against her. It makes her acutely aware of how alone she feels. At some point in her life, Martha realized that, no matter how tight you held onto everything beautiful, everything you thought was yours, it was all going to come to this, being alone. But, she'd rather be alone in her own house than alone in place full of lonely alone old people. It can't end that way.

Candace is speaking to Martha about one her five sisters back in Missouri. She often talks about the relatives she left behind, as if Missouri is another country, and New Hampshire a foreign land. And Martha can always hear the missing in her voice, way deep in the back like tears, though Candace's words sketch family feuds and petty rivalries more than anything else. Martha closes her eyes.

"Well, if you are going to be sleeping beauty, I'll go do errands." Candace's knees crack as she stands up. "You need new bandages for that arm and I'm going to go to Price Chopper, too. I'll be back to get your supper before I go home tonight, okay?" She puts the mail in Martha's hands before she gathers her things, slips on her coat, and shuts the door behind her.

An uneasy quiet settles upon the house. Martha remembers the peace she used to feel when Richard left for work and Raymond for school. Martha would hold a cup of coffee between her hands and rest her hips against the kitchen counter, letting herself melt into the middle of the hush. All that clamored for her attention—household chores, clothes to wash and wring out, volunteer activities with the Ladies Guild—she let go of for a few minutes while the coffee warmed her palms and the silence hummed with promise.

Martha fumbles to open the letters with a silver opener and wonders about Candace's other life, her husband who works at Jake's Auto body, her high school son who gets all A's. She wonders what Candace is sad about and afraid of and if she ever gets to enjoy silence. She'll ask her these things.

Martha opens an envelope with a picture of a gorilla on it. The World Wildlife Fund. Everyone wants money, and Martha sets this request aside to consider later. A bright flyer from a new Chinese restaurant in town makes good reading. Her stomach starts to feel hollow when she reads about the Moo Shu pork and the sautéed shrimp and scallions. She is supposed to be on healthy diet, bland and tasteless is more like it, but Candace will often splash real salad dressing over the greens or hand Martha the salt shaker when she makes a face. Martha picks up a pen next to her phone and circles all the yummy dishes before she sets aside the flyer; maybe she'll convince Candace to order Chinese tonight. The rest of the mail goes into the recycling bag next to her chair.

Martha turns to page four of the paper to read the obituaries. She always reads every word; it is the least she can do, and it's what she will want.

Kate Olmstead Briggs, of Chicago, Formerly of Campton, NH.

Martha feels a tight knot in her chest, feeling panicky and guilty, as if her dream earlier in the day has somehow brought on this news of Kate. Kate, too chicken to climb trees, but who played a wooden recorder and got Martha to follow her anywhere. Kate with the perfect pigtails and sharp brown eyes. Kate with whom Martha made up a secret language, almost set a field on fire, lay in the cemetery after school wondering about all the dead people. Kate her most memorable childhood friend. Dead at the age of 94. In lieu of flowers donations could be sent to Family and Child Services of Chicago.

For the second time, Martha's eyes are hot with tears. Suddenly, she misses Kate terribly, Kate whom she hasn't seen for eighty-two years, but who is as real and alive and young as she was then. How odd that Martha dreamt of her and now this. It could be an omen. Martha drops the paper and places her face in her hands and begins to weep. She is afraid and wishes Candace would hurry and return.

The light has slid off her lap and lies against the far wall near the fichus tree. The room is dim and blurry.

Martha wakes up to the sound of the back door closing and the clicking of heels and the sharpness of lights being snapped on.

"Granny!" Lauren kneels by her chair, the endearing freckles on her nose close enough to touch, and Martha is glad to see her, for the creeping fear did not dissipate with sleep.

"What time is it?" Martha notices that Lauren's hair, in a twist of some sort, is coming undone and wisps are loose about her face.

"Four-thirty. I put the kettle on for tea." Lauren gets up and takes off her high heels and yawns as she heads back to the kitchen.

Martha admires her strong and graceful posture and tries to sit up a little straighter in her chair. She can feel herself stiffening a little in Lauren's presence, though her granddaughter's tiredness softens her a tiny bit. She gathers the fallen newspaper and tries to fold it while Lauren brings in the tea.

Lauren puts a mug for Martha on the side table.

"Candace made coconut macaroons yesterday. You might find them on the counter." Martha picks up her tea and a bit sloshes on her afghan; she hopes that Lauren doesn't notice the tremor in her arm.

"Ooh, I feel fat. I'm trying to lose the last five pounds now that I'm done nursing." Lauren sits on the couch, unzips her skirt a couple inches and pulls her creamy silk blouse free of the waistband.

"I was hoping you'd bring the baby." Martha feels love akin to pain every time she sees Finn. Not just beautiful, but innocent and pure. What she will miss.

Lauren starts talking about the baby, how Finn tips over when he sits. She has a lovely dimple on her right cheek, just like Raymond, and Martha sees it deepen as she talks.

"Let's see that arm, Gran." Lauren unclips her hair from its twist and barrettes it back before coming to Martha's side. Martha sips her tea. Lauren forgot to put in sugar. She has so much on her mind, Martha shouldn't blame her for not remembering how she takes her tea, but somehow this looms as an offense. Candace would not have forgotten. Lauren takes Martha's mug, sets it aside and kneels down.

"Oh, it's fine. Candace's been taking good care of it." Martha clasps her hand around opposite wrist, holding her sweater down so Lauren can't pull it up.

"I told Dad I'd call him tonight with the details." Lauren slips a finger under Martha's and pries, gently, her hand off her wrist. She rolls up the soft blue cashmere with her cool fingers. Martha holds her breath as Lauren peels back the adhesive tape and gauze.

"You poor thing, that is terrible looking." They both survey the purple and green bruise spreading out around the cut.

"It is hardly life threatening." Martha yanks her arm back and pulls the shawl around it.

Lauren stands up abruptly and Martha braces herself.

"I just can't do it all," Lauren says, waving her hand to take in the room and Martha. Martha's hand itches to slap her. "Good Lord girl, this is not about you!" Martha says.

The back door bangs open and Martha can see Candace edging in with full arms.

"It's Candace! With Chinese!"

Lauren rolls her eyes and strides off into the kitchen.

Martha looks at spot on the table where the flyer for the new Chinese restaurant was; Candace must have come back from her errands while she was sleeping and taken it off to the restaurant to order.

Dishes clink and silverware rattles and the smell of shrimp and spices warms up the house. Martha's mouth begins to water.

"Granny's arm looks terrible." Martha can hear Lauren's conspiratorial whisper even though they are in the kitchen. Really, she is rather vain about her hearing and hates being with the old people who completely garble what's being said.

"The doctor says she's going to live—or, at least, it won't be the arm," Candace says. On a tray, Candace brings a plate heaped with steaming rice and shiny bright food; it is much more than she can eat, and Candace knows that. Candace places the tray on Martha's lap with a wink.

Candace settles into the couch with her own plate of food. Lauren, who followed Candace from the kitchen, stands in the middle of the room with her arms tight around her.

"Help yourself, Lauren." Candace chuckles as she stabs a piece of chicken with water chestnuts.

"Candace, she can't eat that, it'll kill her." Lauren turns to Candace, who calmly chews. .

"Oh, Lauren. Why not die happy? I say die happy!" This from Candace. Martha puts a bit of shrimp between her teeth and bites.

"Did you at least ask for it without MSG? That stuff is toxic."

Martha wonders if she should take Lauren on her lap and pat her hair and let her play with her bracelets; she looks like a girl with the weight of the world on her thin shoulders.

Martha nibbles the shrimp, grateful for small things like her own teeth and a tongue that still yearns for flavorful things. She closes her eyes to savor the taste and hears Lauren sigh.

"Oh for Christ's sake, you two," Lauren says. She slumps off to the kitchen, shirt tails dangling.

Martha looks at Candace who is heartily engaged with the food on her plate and doesn't look up. She wonders what Lauren is doing in the kitchen. Buttoning up her shearling coat? Standing at the sink plotting how to get Martha to move out? Martha is feeling full after only a few bites; a little goes a long way now, but she feels good and warm inside.

Lauren comes back to the doorway, a saucer size plate balanced on one palm. With her fingers she picks up a dripping stalk of broccoli. Candace looks at Martha with a wink.

"I saw that Candace," Lauren says.

"What? What?" Candace pretends innocence.

"Come sit with us for heaven's sake, Lauren," Martha waggles her hand at floor next to her chair.

Lauren hesitates and licks some sauce off her fingers.

"I have to get home soon, to the baby. And nothing's been resolved." She looks right into Martha's eyes. Martha is drawn in and feels like she can see down into Lauren's heart—like she can see those little chambers where all Lauren's loves and responsibilities lie.

Oh dear lord she will miss those eyes, that heart.

"Just for a moment, sit with me."

Lauren sits down on the floor near Martha, her saucer of food in her palm. She leans back against the chair, so close that Martha can reach out and touch her if she wants.

Candace gets up, "I'm thirsty. Anybody else want water? Wine? Beer?" She heads toward the kitchen.

"Water, please, Candace," whispers Lauren.

Lauren shivers and Martha pulls her shawl of one thousand Hail Marys from around her shoulders and drapes it over Lauren. Lauren takes her hand and presses it against her own warm cheek.

A rush of love expands in Martha's chest, and she prays that this moment will go on and on, with her palm against Lauren's face, with the scratching of the crab apple against the black window and the whoosh of the heat coming on and the sound of Candace singing in the kitchen while the water runs.

About the Author

In addition to writing short stories, Victoria Fish is pursuing her Masters of Social Work. Her stories have appeared in numerous literary magazines, including *Hunger Mountain, Slow Trains, Wild River Review,* and *Literary Mama.* She lives with her husband and three boys in the hills of Vermont. *A Brief Moment of Weightlessness* is her first book. She can be found at *www.vickyfish.com.*

Other Recent Titles from Mayapple Press:

Susana H. Case, *4 Rms w Vu*, 2014
        Paper, 72pp, $15.95 plus s&h
        ISBN 978-1-936419-39-5
Elizabeth Genovise, *A Different Harbor*, 2014
        Paper, 76pp, $15.95 plus s&h
        ISBN 978-1-936419-38-8
Marjorie Stelmach, *Without Angels*, 2014
        Paper, 74pp, $15.95 plus s&h
        ISBN 978-1-936419-37-1
David Lunde, *The Grandson of Heinrich Schliemann & Other Truths and Fictions*, 2014
        Paper, 62pp, $14.95 plus s&h
        ISBN 978-1-936419-36-4
Eleanor Lerman, *Strange Life*, 2014
        Paper, 90pp, $15.95 plus s&h
        ISBN 978-1-936419-35-7
Sally Rosen Kindred, *Book of Asters*, 2014
        Paper, 74pp, $15.95 plus s&h
        ISBN 978-1-936419-34-0
Gretchen Primack, *Doris' Red Spaces*, 2014
        Paper, 74pp, $15.95 plus s&h
        ISBN 978-1-936419-33-3
Stephen Lewandowski, *Under Foot*, 2014
        Paper, 80pp, $15.95 plus s&h
        ISBN 978-1-936419-32-6
Hilma Contreras (Judith Kerman, Tr.), *Between Two Silences/ Entre Dos Silencios*, 2013
        Paper, 126pp, $16.95 plus s&h
        ISBN 978-1-936419-31-9
Helen Ruggieri & Linda Underhill, Eds., *Written on Water: Writings about the Allegheny River*, 2013
        Paper, 108pp, $19.95 plus s&h (includes Bonus CD)
        ISBN 978-1-936419-30-2
Don Cellini, *Candidates for sainthood and other sinners/ Aprendices de santo y otros pecadores*, 2013
        Paper, 62pp, $14.95 plus s&h
        ISBN 978-1-936419-29-6
Gerry LaFemina, *Notes for the Novice Ventriloquist*, 2013
        Paper, 78pp, $15.95 plus s&h
        ISBN 978-1-936419-28-9

For a complete catalog of Mayapple Press publications, please visit our website at *www.mayapplepress.com*. Books can be ordered direct from our website with secure on-line payment using PayPal, or by mail (check or money order). Or order through your local bookseller.